Acting Edition

MW01089467

... the
Natalie
Portmans

by C.A. Johnson

‖SAMUEL FRENCH‖

FOR PRODUCTION INQUIRIES
UNITED STATES AND CANADA
info@concordtheatricals.com
1-866-979-0447

UNITED KINGDOM AND EUROPE
licensing@concordtheatricals.co.uk
020-7054-7298

Each title is subject to availability from Concord Theatricals Corp., depending upon country of performance. Please be aware that *ALL THE NATALIE PORTMANS* may not be licensed by Concord Theatricals Corp. in your territory. Professional and amateur producers should contact the nearest Concord Theatricals Corp. office or licensing partner to verify availability.

This work is published by Samuel French, an imprint of Concord Theatricals Corp.

No one shall make any changes in this title(s) for the purpose of production. No part of this book may be reproduced, stored in a retrieval system, scanned, uploaded, or transmitted in any form, by any means, now known or yet to be invented, including mechanical, electronic, digital, photocopying, recording, videotaping, or otherwise, without the prior written permission of the publisher. No one shall share this title(s), or any part of this title(s), through any social media or file hosting websites.

For all inquiries regarding motion picture, television, online/digital and other media rights, please contact Concord Theatricals Corp.

MUSIC AND THIRD-PARTY MATERIALS USE NOTE

Licensees are solely responsible for obtaining formal written permission from copyright owners to use copyrighted music and/or other copyrighted third-party materials (e.g., artworks, logos) in the performance of this play and are strongly cautioned to do so. If no such permission is obtained by the licensee, then the licensee must use only original music and materials that the licensee owns and controls. Licensees are solely responsible and liable for clearances of all third-party copyrighted materials, including without limitation music, and shall indemnify the copyright owners of the play(s) and their licensing agent, Concord Theatricals Corp., against any costs, expenses, losses and liabilities arising from the use of such copyrighted third-party materials by licensees. For music, please contact the appropriate music licensing authority in your territory for the rights to any incidental music.

IMPORTANT BILLING AND CREDIT REQUIREMENTS

If you have obtained performance rights to this title, please refer to your licensing agreement for important billing and credit requirements.

ALL THE NATALIE PORTMANS premiered Off-Broadway at MCC Theater in New York City in February 2020. The performance was directed by Kate Whoriskey, with sets by Donyale Werle, costumes by Jennifer Moeller, lighting by Stacey Derosier, sound by Sinan Refik Zafar, and props by Alexander Wylie. The production stage manager was Alexandra Hall. The cast was as follows:

KEYONNA	Kara Young
SAMUEL	Joshua Boone
CHANTEL	Renika Wiliams
OVETTA	Montego Glover
NATALIE PORTMAN	Elise Kibler
EPPS	Raphael Peacock

CHARACTERS

KEYONNA – sixteen, smart, lonely, a dreamer

SAMUEL – eighteen, exceedingly kind, a high-school dropout, a fixer

CHANTEL – seventeen, very pretty, very afraid, but quick

OVETTA – mid-forties, a hotel worker, recovering alcoholic, trying

NATALIE PORTMAN – white, ageless, the Academy Award-winning actress (sort of)

EPPS – upstairs neighbor, landlord, alcoholic (heard but not seen)

SETTING

Northeast Washington, D.C.

TIME

2009

AUTHOR'S NOTES

A Few Notes on Natalie

It's not important that the actress look like Natalie Portman too closely.
It's also not important that she too obviously emulates the real woman or her various roles.

She is a manifestation of Keyonna's inner psyche, which serves a purpose that, though tangential to the given role being cited, is wholly its own thing.

In short: play around.

About the Dream Board

It's on a literal wall inside the house and visible to the audience.

It should contain photos of actresses of note from the late '80s to the early 2000s. They are mostly white, but maybe there's a Sanaa Lathan here and a Nia Long there – definitely a Halle Berry somewhere.

You get it.

For the Actors

Some pauses are long. Some are short bumps where characters are choosing their woods carefully. Feel it out.

— indicates the character being interrupted

... indicates searching

– indicates a thing left unsaid but likely physically delivered (not necessarily a pause)

ALL CAPS indicate emphasis (not necessarily volume)

// indicates the start of the next line (with overlap)

ACT I

Scene One

(A basement apartment. We see a living area, kitchen, two closed doors that lead to bedrooms, and a short hallway leading to a bathroom. This space is filled with way too much furniture, the amount of furniture that screams history and family all scrunched into foreign territory.)

(One wall of the room is notably covered in magazine cutouts of famous female movie stars [think cover photos, ads, the whole gamut]. This wall is intentional and well cared for with space left for more photos.)*

*(There is also music coming from one of the bedrooms, something along the lines of Ginuwine or Tyrese.** After a moment, the music abruptly stops, and the bedroom door bursts open. CHANTEL enters. She's pulling on a shirt and dragging a backpack.)*

SAMUEL. *(Offstage.)* Ay! Chantel!

---

*A license to produce *All the Natalie Portmans* does not include a license to publicly display any third-party or copyrighted images. Licensees must acquire rights for any copyrighted images or create their own.

**A license to produce *All the Natalie Portmans* does not include a performance license for any third-party or copyrighted music. Licensees should create an original composition or use music in the public domain. For further information, please see the Music and Third-Party Materials Use Note on page iii.

SAMUEL. *(Offstage.)* Chantel!

> *(**CHANTEL** heads for the door, just as **SAMUEL** enters. He too is pulling on a garment, likely boxers.)*

Wait!

Can't you just wait?

CHANTEL. For what?

SAMUEL. For me to catch up with you.

Duh.

> *(**CHANTEL** is not amused. She heads for the front door.)*

Shit. Hold up, Chan.

Seriously hold up.

> *(**SAMUEL** grabs hold of **CHANTEL**'s hand. She pauses despite herself.)*

My bad, aight?

CHANTEL. That's all you got to say to me, Sam?

SAMUEL. ...What else you want me to say?

CHANTEL. How 'bout sorry I made you come all this way, Chantel.

Sorry I made you miss your free period.

Sorry I got you all hot, and I ain't even got no rubbers.

SAMUEL. But I do got rubbers.

I just showed you the box.

CHANTEL. Not from no 1980 you don't.

SAMUEL. What's wrong with 1980?

CHANTEL. Condoms expire, Samuel.

SAM. Don't no condoms expire.

CHANTEL. They do. They got expiration dates right on the wrapper.

SAMUEL. –

CHANTEL. I mean it. Go look.

You so fuckin' smart go read it.

> (**SAMUEL** *pauses and then exits into the bedroom. After a beat, he returns, holding a condom wrapper up to the light.*)

SAMUEL. Damn.

CHANTEL. Exactly.

> (*Again,* **CHANTEL** *goes to leave.*)

SAMUEL. But hold up. Come on, Chan.

It's other stuff we could do.

We got thirty minutes fo' Keyonna get home.

CHANTEL. And? What that got to do with me?

SAMUEL. Well, don't you wanna just play a lil bit?

Cuddle up and shit?

CHANTEL. No.

I don't.

SAMUEL. Why not?

CHANTEL. Because I ain't your girlfriend, Samuel.

SAMUEL. Yeah you *say* that —

CHANTEL. No, I *mean* that.

It's a difference.

> (*A small pause.*)

SAMUEL. Like I ain't worth your time?

CHANTEL. Here we go with the woe is me shit —

SAMUEL. No. No. I wanna know.

You think you too good for me or somethin'?

CHANTEL. Why you always gotta be so melodramatic, young?

SAMUEL. 'Cause.

CHANTEL. 'Cause why?

SAMUEL. 'Cause you keep frontin' like I'm just some dude from round the way. Even though we both know better.

We know each other, Chantel.

CHANTEL. Okay. So?

SAMUEL. So you can't jus' be like let's smash one minute, and then act like I ain't nobody the next.

CHANTEL. I ain't never in my life used the word smash and you know it —

SAMUEL. That's beside the point, mo.

How are you chill with walkin' round here like I ain't nothin' or nobody?

Like I'm garbage?

CHANTEL. You are not garbage, Sam.

SAMUEL. I'm not?

CHANTEL. No.

SAMUEL. Then what am I?

If I ain't your boyfriend, and I ain't garbage, what that make me?

CHANTEL. –

SAMUEL. –

CHANTEL. My friend, aight?

It make you my friend.

SAMUEL. Your friend.

Okay.

CHANTEL. Samuel —

SAMUEL. It's whatever —

CHANTEL. Sam, look at me.

(He does.)

This is fun. We have fun.

We laugh, and we chill, and we *smash*.

But that's it, right?

We agreed. That's it.

SAMUEL. I'on remember agreein' to that.

CHANTEL. Yes, you do.

(A pause.)

It's better this way.

SAMUEL. Better for who though, Chan?

CHANTEL. Better for me.

SAMUEL. –

CHANTEL. Is that still cool?

SAMUEL. –

CHANTEL. Sam?

SAMUEL. Yeah. That's cool.

CHANTEL. Good.

'Cause if you go buy some more rubbers, I just might stop by tomorrow.

SAMUEL. Oh yeah?

CHANTEL. Maybe.

If I'm in the mood.

SAMUEL. Man, you play too much.

CHANTEL. I play just enough.

> *(She kisses him. A tease. Then she moves toward the door.)*

I gotta go.

SAMUEL. Oh, so you just gon' leave a brotha hangin'?

CHANTEL. Goodbye, Samuel.

SAMUEL. You stone cold, you know that?

> *(**CHANTEL** pulls open the front door and finds **KEYONNA** there. She stops short.)*

CHANTEL. Hey, Key.

KEYONNA. Hey.

> *(**KEYONNA** moves past **CHANTEL** and into the apartment.)*

CHANTEL. Uh...I got homework.

I'll see y'all later.

KEYONNA. Later.

SAMUEL. Bye!

> *(**CHANTEL** exits. **KEYONNA** drops her backpack and plops down on the couch.)*

You ain't supposed to be home for another half.

KEYONNA. So, I'm early.

SAMUEL. So that ain't cool, Keyonna. You gon' be early, text me.

Don't just be rollin' up.

KEYONNA. Why not? You clearly ain't get none.

SAMUEL. Don't you worry 'bout what I got.

KEYONNA. I don't know why you goin' after Chantel anyway. She out your league, mo.

SAMUEL. Who league she in then?

Yours?

KEYONNA. Did I say anything like that?

SAMUEL. No, but she is vicious.

And yo' gay ass ain't blind.

KEYONNA. Yeah well, my gay ass also been knowin' Chantel my whole life.

So you can keep all that "she sexy" noise to yourself.

SAMUEL. Whatchu mean? I known her just as long as you, and I can still admit she a dime.

KEYONNA. A dime a dozen.

SAMUEL. Damn it's like that?

KEYONNA. It ain't like nothing, nigga. Shit.

Can you just go put some clothes on.

Don't nobody wanna see your knocked knees.

> (**SAMUEL** *tosses something at* **KEYONNA.** *She instinctively hurls it back, but before it can land,* **SAMUEL** *exits into his bedroom.*)

Punk!

> (**KEYONNA** *reclines on the sofa and pulls a stack of fashion magazines from her backpack.*)

SAMUEL. *(Offstage.)* You bring any food?

KEYONNA. Your momma bring any food?

(**KEYONNA** *picks out one of the magazines and begins to flip through it.*)

SAMUEL. *(Offstage.)* How was school?

KEYONNA. I went to my classes.

If that's what you askin'.

SAMUEL. *(Offstage.)* What else would I be askin', Keyonna?

KEYONNA. School was whatever.

(**SAMUEL** *re-enters, now clad in bottoms and a top. He proceeds to make himself a bowl of cereal.*)

SAMUEL. You wanna try that again?

KEYONNA. Man, here you go —

SAMUEL. Just answer the question, Key —

KEYONNA. Bruh, why are you doin' so much? —

SAMUEL. In full sentences.

Put all them big ass words of yours to use —

KEYONNA. Fuck. Fine. School was fine.

We took another practice test in AP Bio and I got a four.

Film class was baller. As usual.

And in AP Lang we read a bunch of borin' ass rhetorical essays.

That enough sentences for you?

SAMUEL. How was AP Calc?

KEYONNA. Fine.

SAMUEL. Did you go, Keyonna?

KEYONNA. Yes, Sam. I went to calculus.

SAMUEL. You sure about that?

...'Cause you know they installed that new system.

I get a robo-text when you skip.

KEYONNA. So, if you already know the answer, why you even askin'?

SAMUEL. 'Cause that shit ain't cool, Key.

You go to that charter school for a reason, remember?

(**KEYONNA** *flips through her magazine.*)

SAMUEL. Chantel say you been hangin' by yourself a lot.

KEYONNA. Did she also say why she all up in my business?

SAMUEL. She in it 'cause I asked her to be, Keyonna.

I asked her to look out for you.

KEYONNA. Ughhhhhh —

SAMUEL. Not that I had to ask all that hard.

You know how much she care about you —

KEYONNA. I don't need nobody lookin' out for me, okay.

SAMUEL. Oh yeah?

KEYONNA. *Yes.*

(*A small pause.*)

SAMUEL. Nobody been fuckin' witchu right? Or like bullyin' you —

KEYONNA. I'm a lesbian, Samuel.

Not a leper.

Don't nobody care —

SAMUEL. *(Firm.)* Of course, they care, Keyonna.

KEYONNA. –

SAMUEL. And what I'm asking you...is if you good?

KEYONNA. I skipped calc 'cause it's easy, Sam.

Not 'cause nobody is bullyin' me.

Kill with all that.

> (**KEYONNA** *returns to her magazine.* **SAMUEL**
> *crosses into the living room and considers the*
> *wall of photos.)*

SAMUEL. You runnin' outta room on this wall, you know.

KEYONNA. So?

SAMUEL. So you might wanna slow your roll?

Or take some down.

KEYONNA. Can't take 'em down.

SAMUEL. Why not?

KEYONNA. It's called a dream board, Sam.

You take any of 'em down that's like throwin' away a
dream.

SAMUEL. Some of these are old though.

Look. Like you don't need Winona Ryder up here.

She ain't made a movie in how long?

KEYONNA. She gon' make a comeback.

SAMUEL. Says who?

KEYONNA. Says the nigga who gon' put her back on the map.

SAMUEL. And you that nigga?

KEYONNA. Screenplay gon' be so tight, all them white folks
gon' forget she ever stole from that department store.

SAMUEL. Ain't nobody forgettin' that, Key.

Shit was hilarious.

KEYONNA. You wanna bet?

SAMUEL. No, I want you to slow down.

Ma ain't gon' like if you take up another one of her walls with this mess —

KEYONNA. *(Firm.)* It ain't mess, Sam.

...Anyway, I know better than to take up another wall.

I don't wanna fight with Ma, just as much as she don't wanna fight with me.

> (**KEYONNA** *stops on a page in the magazine and holds it up to the light, judging it.*)

SAMUEL. Who you find?

KEYONNA. Kate Holmes.

SAM. Off *Dawson's Creek*?

KEYONNA. Yep.

A full-page spread.

SAMUEL. Like she cute or some shit?

KEYONNA. Whatchu mean "like she cute"?

SAMUEL. I mean...she ain't cute.

KEYONNA. Boy bye.

SAMUEL. She ain't.

KEYONNA. Who you think is cute then?

SAMUEL. Kiki Shepard.

KEYONNA. Off the Apollo?

SAMUEL. Yep.

KEYONNA. But she old as cheese.

SAMUEL. She vintage you mean.

KEYONNA. No, I mean old.

But it ain't like I expect you to have good taste.

SAMUEL. Fuck you I got great taste.

KEYONNA. Liiiikkkee?

SAMUEL. Chantel.

> (**KEYONNA** *returns to her flipping.*)

KEYONNA. Are we already back on Chantel?

SAMUEL. You gotta admit she bad.

KEYONNA. I ain't gotta admit nothin' on that front actually.

SAMUEL. Just trust me, Key.

When Chan come out them jeans I swear —

KEYONNA. Ughhhhhh no. Stop.

SAMUEL. It's like pow! —

KEYONNA. Gahhhhhh Samuel —

SAMUEL. Pa dow! —

KEYONNA. SAM —

SAMUEL. *(Laughing.)* Aight. Aight.

I'll stop.

> (*He is beside himself with laughter.*)

KEYONNA. I hate you.

SAMUEL. You wish you hated me.

> (**KEYONNA** *makes a show of ignoring him for a moment, but then something in the magazine grabs her attention. Her face lights up.*)

Let me guess.

Natalie Portman.

KEYONNA. You know it.

> (**SAMUEL** *grabs a nearby pair of scissors and holds them out to her.* **KEYONNA** *takes them with a smile and begins cutting out the image.*)

SAMUEL. You really think she all that?

KEYONNA. I'm tellin' you, Sam.

She the best in the game right now.

SAMUEL. Better than Charlize Theron?

KEYONNA. Well, no but that ain't even a fair comparison.

They wouldn't even be offered the same parts.

SAMUEL. Still. Half this damn wall used to be Charlize.

KEYONNA. What's your point?

SAMUEL. How come Natalie get to be half the damn dream board?

KEYONNA. *Because.*

If I can write a role for Natalie.

I can write a role for anybody.

I mean...it'd have to be somebody smart, but sweet, and kinda sexy in an untouchable way. Like...one part princess...one part stripper...one part Russian spy.

You know?

SAMUEL. Not really.

KEYONNA. Hollywood is full of beautiful, talented women, Sam.

And I see that. I honor it.

And someday I'ma make mad money exploiting the hell out of it.

Natalie is my ticket.

SAMUEL. Still. If it was me, I'd be putting up more Gabrielle Union. A lil' more Sanaa Lathan.

Plus, you ain't even got Nia Long up here.

KEYONNA. That's 'cause my tastes is varied, nigga.

Also, what you call that right there?

SAMUEL. I call that one picture of Whoopi Goldberg.

KEYONNA. Whoopi is a bombass actor.

SAMUEL. In what?

KEYONNA. *THE COLOR PURPLE*!

What are you even askin' me right now?

SAMUEL. *(Noticing the time.)* AightAight. Let me not get caught up in all this with you again.

KEYONNA. Why? 'Cause you know I'm a genius?

SAMUEL. No, 'cause I gotta go to work.

KEYONNA. Already?

But you said you would watch *A Walk to Remember* with me.

SAMUEL. We can watch it tomorrow.

Lee asked me to come in early to talk about some stuff.

*(**SAMUEL** exits into his room.)*

KEYONNA. Since when do Lee got a reason to talk to you off the clock?

SAMUEL. *(Offstage.)* I'on know. He been on one all week.

And about little shit like how I towel-dry the glasses wrong.

KEYONNA. So not talk in a bad way?

SAMUEL. *(Offstage.)* Nah. Just in a Lee way.

You know how he be sycin' shit. 'Specially when it come to me.

"Yo' daddy woulda said this," "Yo' daddy woulda done it like that." "I know I ain't your daddy but," and on and on.

(*A small pause.*)

You aight to feed yourself?

KEYONNA. You leave any cereal in the box?

(**SAMUEL** *re-enters, ready to go.*)

SAMUEL. You ain't got no money for the carryout?

KEYONNA. Where I was gon' get it from? You?

SAMUEL. From Ma.

KEYONNA. I ain't even seen Ma.

SAMUEL. Whatchu mean you ain't seen her?

Since when?

KEYONNA. Since Monday. You seen her?

SAMUEL. Nah. But I figure she just ate her lunch at the hotel all week.

KEYONNA. She never eat her lunch at the hotel, Sam.

SAMUEL. Well, you ain't tell me she ain't been home.

(*A small pause.*)

She pay Epps yesterday though, right?

KEYONNA. I don't know.

(*Another pause.*)

SAMUEL. Let me get your phone.

(**KEYONNA** *pulls a phone from her pocket and hands it to him.*)

KEYONNA. I'm down to like twelve minutes, Sam.

SAMUEL. I know. I won't waste 'em.

> *(He dials a number. **KEYONNA** watches him. They wait for many moments, holding their breath. And then he hangs up.)*

Voicemail.

KEYONNA. That don't mean nothin'.

You know she can't answer when she on shift.

SAMUEL. –

KEYONNA. Sam, it might not even mean nothin' —

SAMUEL. Just let me know if she call you back, aight?

KEYONNA. Okay.

SAMUEL. And if she show up, don't let her leave without givin' you the cash.

KEYONNA. I won't.

> *(**SAMUEL** digs in a pocket and removes a bill.)*

SAMUEL. Here.

Get yourself something to eat.

> *(**KEYONNA** takes it.)*

See you in the mornin', Key.

...And sorry about your movie.

KEYONNA. It's cool.

See you.

> *(**SAMUEL** exits. **KEYONNA** stares at the closed door for a moment, but then remembers the cutout image. She picks it up and crosses to her board. She lovingly moves a few photos*

around, trying to find the right configuration. When she finally finds a space for it, she pins the cutout with a tack, takes a step back, and peers at the wall in its entirety.)

Nah.

(She snatches the photo down, unsatisfied. As she does this, **NATALIE PORTMAN** *appears. She's dressed as a ballerina, something that generally evokes her character in* Black Swan. **KEYONNA** *watches in pure delight as* **NATALIE** *bounds toward her, takes the cutout, crosses to the board, and pins it in a new location. They both take in her choice.)*

NATALIE. Perfect.

*(**NATALIE** smiles at **KEYONNA**, and maybe for the first time all scene, **KEYONNA** exhales.)*

Now what?

*(**KEYONNA** grabs a magazine, and they both peer excitedly at its content.)*

(Lights shift.)

Scene Two

(The apartment later that night. The room is dark. **KEYONNA** *lies on the sofa, watching a movie. She's enthralled. After a pause,* **OVETTA** *enters through the front door. She wears a hotel maid's uniform and immediately starts shedding layers. As she does this, the film plays through a key dramatic scene.* Both* **OVETTA** *and* **KEYONNA** *take it in, but only* **KEYONNA** *is very emotional. Then the scene ends.* **KEYONNA** *wipes at her eyes.)*

OVETTA. *A Walk to Remember* again?

KEYONNA. You know it.

OVETTA. Hm.

*(***OVETTA** *joins* **KEYONNA** *on the sofa. Though she's hiding it well, she is a tiny bit tipsy.)*

Did she fall for him yet?

KEYONNA. She about to.

(They watch.)

OVETTA. I like her I think.

Can't sing worth a damn.

But maybe she better off as a actor.

KEYONNA. Right?

(A pause.)

---

*A license to produce *All the Natalie Portmans* does not include a performance license for any third-party or copyrighted recordings or videos. Licensees must acquire rights for any copyrighted recordings or videos or create their own. Unless rights are acquired, audiences cannot hear or see any recordings or videos from *A Walk to Remember*.

OVETTA. You already eat?

>   (**KEYONNA** *nods.*)

You full?

>   (**KEYONNA** *shrugs.*)

I can get in there and cook something, Keyonna.

If you want me to.

KEYONNA. It's two a.m., Ma.

OVETTA. Still I can —

KEYONNA. Ain't nothing in there to cook.

>   (*Another pause.*)

OVETTA. Well. If you get hungry, I can walk to the carryout.

Get you some chicken and fried rice.

Only if you want it.

KEYONNA. I appreciate that, Ma.

OVETTA. I appreciate you, babygirl.

>   (*They watch the movie. The music is really swelling now.* **OVETTA** *laughs.*)

Here she go, cryin'.

What she cryin' for?

KEYONNA. She don't wanna fall in love with him.

OVETTA. Yeah, but remind me why.

KEYONNA. Well Landon is like the bad boy in town, right?

---

*A license to produce *All the Natalie Portmans* does not include a performance license for any third-party or copyrighted recordings or videos. Licensees must acquire rights for any copyrighted recordings or videos or create their own. Unless rights are acquired, audiences cannot hear or see any recordings or videos from *A Walk to Remember*.

And he's in love with Jamie, the preacher's daughter, which is mad complicated.

And even though Landon can see that Jamie likes him, she still won't give him the time of day.

OVETTA. Mm-hm.

KEYONNA. But what Landon don't know is that Jamie is fully aware of her emotions.

She just sayin' no because she don't know how to tell him the real, deep-down truth.

OVETTA. Rightttt. Right.

She got cancer.

KEYONNA. Exactly.

She don't wanna hurt him.

Or like die on him I guess.

(A small pause.)

OVETTA. This is some dumb shit.

KEYONNA. It's not dumb.

OVETTA. It is, Keyonna.

I don't know how you even sit here watchin' this madness all day.

KEYONNA. I don't watch it all day.

I go to school, remember? I do my homework. I play my part.

And then, as a reward, I get to watch whatever I want.

OVETTA. Yeah, but what's so wrong with watchin' *Set It Off*?

Or *Boyz N The Hood*?

Or *Soul Food*?

Somethin' good.

KEYONNA. I do watch those movies —

OVETTA. Then put one of them on now.

Woman come home to her house, lease she can do is watch a program she like.

(**KEYONNA** *stands. She turns off the movie and switches out the DVD over the next.*)

I don't know why your father even started you with all this mess in the first place.

First time he showed you *Steel Magnolias* I knew it was gon' be trouble.

Sally Field threw herself down over that grave and child you just lost it.

Cried for a week 'bout that damn movie.

I had to put on *The Pelican Brief* just to show you Julia Roberts was still alive.

Look, Keyonna I say. There she is right there.

And you just look and look 'til it make sense to you.

"She alright."

"Your friends is alright."

KEYONNA. It was a convincin' movie.

OVETTA. But you wasn't exactly cryin' about the movie was you?

KEYONNA. –

OVETTA. Was you? —

KEYONNA. I don't even remember none of this, Ma —

OVETTA. You was cryin' 'cause you thought a white woman was dead.

It was the end of your lil' world, child.

KEYONNA. Or it was just a moment.

OVETTA. Ain't nothin' just a moment for you, Keyonna.
Not ever.

>   *(A pause.)*

Talk to me about this sexuality shit.

KEYONNA. What? No.

OVETTA. No. No. I wanna talk about it.
I wanna understand it.

KEYONNA. Understand what?

OVETTA. You a lesbian, right?
That's what you say.

KEYONNA. That's what I know.

OVETTA. So talk me through it.

KEYONNA. –

OVETTA. How long you known you like cat?

>   *(This question hangs in the air, and then*
>   **OVETTA** *laughs.)*

Cat.

I crack myself up.

>   *(**KEYONNA** takes this in and then steps away*
>   *from the TV.)*

KEYONNA. I'm goin' to bed, Ma.

OVETTA. No, you ain't. Not when I'm in the middle of
talkin' to you.

KEYONNA. You talkin' at me, actually.

OVETTA. I'm your momma.
I can talk however I want —

KEYONNA. Yeah well how about you try talkin' to me when you're sober, hunh?

How 'bout that?

OVETTA. I am sober —

KEYONNA. Yeah right.

OVETTA. Keyonna, I am —

KEYONNA. DON'T LIE TO ME, MA.

...Not about this.

> *(A pause.)*

OVETTA. Aight. I won't lie.

I had me a drink.

KEYONNA. Was it upstairs with Mr. Epps?

OVETTA. Epps ain't the only way I can find liquor, Keyonna.

The world is big —

KEYONNA. Did you drink with him tonight or not?

OVETTA. Yes, I did.

KEYONNA. And?

OVETTA. And what?

KEYONNA. Did you also pay him the rent while you were up there?

Because Sam needs to know.

OVETTA. I am not a child, Keyonna.

You ain't gon' talk to me like this in my own house —

KEYONNA. Just answer the goddamn question, Ma.

> *(A loaded pause. If **OVETTA** had a Momma-gun, she'd be loading it.)*

You been gone three days, you know.

Ain't call.

Ain't explain.

Ain't even check in.

OVETTA. You grown.

You don't need checkin' in on —

KEYONNA. Yeah, but you do.

You need a world of checkin' in on.

OVETTA. –

KEYONNA. You were doin' so good.

We all were.

Why you gotta fuck it all up now?

OVETTA. You gon' stop cussin' in my presence lil' girl —

KEYONNA. We worry, Ma.

We get scared.

Can't you see that?

OVETTA. I *see* that if you don't watch how you talkin' to me I might have to come 'cross your face —

KEYONNA. And there she is.

The Ovetta I know.

One step away from another bottle.

Two steps away from a slap.

Three steps away from lettin' everybody down —

> (**OVETTA** *crosses the space between them and grabs* **KEYONNA** *like she's a rag doll. She leans in, menacing.*)

OVETTA. Make that the last time you talk stupid to me.

You hear?

KEYONNA. –

OVETTA. Do-you-hear-me?

KEYONNA. I hear you.

> (**OVETTA** *releases* **KEYONNA**. *Maybe she even regrets it, but she'd never let that show.)*

OVETTA. I broke my back to get us this apartment.

Your father left this world and damn near took our whole livelihood wit' him, but I found a way. Me.

So if I see fit to work a double, I'm gon' work it.

And if I see fit to sit and have me a nightcap with Mr. Epps, I'ma do that too.

'Cause it's my right.

Real world ain't like them movies, Keyonna.

I ain't gotta listen to your mouth.

> (**OVETTA** *exits.* **KEYONNA** *massages her cheek for a beat, trying to come down from this moment. But then she crosses to the dream board and begins to pull various cutouts down. It's a bit unclear whether she's rearranging them or angrily destroying her artwork, but somewhere in the middle of this,* **NATALIE PORTMAN** *appears. She wears headphones and quirky, girl-next-door pastels [something that evokes her character Sam from* Garden State*]. She watches* **KEYONNA** *for a beat.)*

NATALIE. Why are you doing that?

> (**KEYONNA** *startles, but when she sees* **NATALIE***, she relaxes a bit.)*

KEYONNA. Shit.

Yo, you scared the hell out of me.

NATALIE. Why are you taking them down?

KEYONNA. We talked about this, Natalie.

Don't be creepin'.

Announce yourself.

NATALIE. Announcement: I've arrived.

Now, why are you destroying your board?

KEYONNA. Because.

> (**KEYONNA** *focuses on the wall, her movements still frenzied.* **NATALIE** *watches for a moment, but then she crosses to* **KEYONNA.**)

NATALIE. Keyonna, stop.

KEYONNA. Stop what?

NATALIE. Just...

> (**NATALIE** *stops* **KEYONNA**'s *hands. A beat. Then she lifts the pair of headphones from around her neck and places them on* **KEYONNA**'s *head. A tiny beat as* **NATALIE** *toggles on an iPhone and selects a song. First* **KEYONNA** *just looks at* **NATALIE**. *But then she listens to the song. She likes it.* **NATALIE** *smiles at her and slowly begins to do a dance – something goofy and adorable that evokes the scene from* Garden State. **KEYONNA** *takes this in for a beat.* **NATALIE** *finishes the dance with a flourish. Then she crosses to* **KEYONNA**. *She takes her face in her hands.* **KEYONNA** *exhales.*)

> (*Lights out.*)

Scene Three

(The next morning. **KEYONNA** *is fast asleep on the sofa. After a beat, we hear shouting outside and the raised voices of two men. One voice becomes clear. It's* **SAMUEL**. *He's right outside.)*

SAMUEL. *(Offstage.)* You gon' get your money aight?

(Something inaudible is yelled back.)

(Offstage.) Jus' keep all that fuckin' yelling on your stoop and not ours.

(The front door opens. **SAMUEL** *is visible now. The* **MAN** *outside is still yelling. It's more clear.)*

MAN. *(Offstage.)* Like I tol' yo' ho-ass momma.

I ain't runnin' no goddamn charity —

SAMUEL. *(Suddenly and with venom.)* SAY ONE MORE FUCKING WORD ABOUT MY MOTHER, EPPS!

JUST ONE.

I DARE YOU.

(A pause. **KEYONNA** *stirs on the sofa.)*

MAN. *(Offstage.)* Just get my money.

(The sound of a door slamming. **SAMUEL** *takes a breath, then enters the apartment.* **KEYONNA** *is awake.* **SAMUEL** *closes the door and takes her in.)*

SAMUEL. Ain't you supposed to be waitin' for the bus right now?

KEYONNA. My head hurt.

It's been poundin' all mornin'.

SAMUEL. I ain't ask 'bout all that.

   I ask why you ain't waitin' on the H-8?

KEYONNA. I jus' tole you, Sam —

SAMUEL. I ain't got time for your shit this morning, Key.

KEYONNA. What shit? I jus' don't feel good —

SAMUEL. First Ma with her mess. Now you slackin' too —

KEYONNA. Don't lump me in with her. It's just one day —

SAMUEL. JUST GET YOUR ASS TO SCHOOL KEYONNA.

   (A pause.)

KEYONNA. Fine.

   Whatever.

   *(**KEYONNA** stands and starts pulling clothes
   from a chest of drawers, but **SAMUEL** really
   takes a look at her now. He softens.)*

SAMUEL. Shit, wait.

KEYONNA. For what?

SAMUEL. Just... I ain't mean to yell at you.

KEYONNA. Yeah well you did so —

SAMUEL. I'm sorry.

   (A small pause.)

KEYONNA. Apology sorta accepted.

   ...

   What's the matter with you anyway?

SAMUEL. Nothin'.

KEYONNA. Don't seem like nothin' —

SAMUEL. Did Ma come home last night, Key?

KEYONNA. Yeah, she did.

SAMUEL. Then why didn't you call me?

KEYONNA. To say what?

SAMUEL. You know the drill, Keyonna.

If she slip, you get her on the phone with me first chance you get.

Don't try to talk to her yourself.

Don't try to reason with her.

None of that.

I handle Ma.

KEYONNA. Yeah well it would've been hard gettin' her to do anything last night, aight.

'Specially gettin' her to do anything I said.

SAMUEL. Why's that?

KEYONNA. Because she was drunk, Sam.

SAMUEL. –

KEYONNA. She was drunk and mean and she was pokin' at me.

SAMUEL. Did she leave you the cash though?

KEYONNA. Of course not.

Soon as I brought it up she got to shuckin' and jivin' 'bout who run this house and how she don't have to answer to me.

SAMUEL. You think the money's gone?

KEYONNA. No tellin' where it went, but it damn sure ain't in her pockets.

(A small pause.)

SAMUEL. You should get to school, Key.

KEYONNA. Not until we got a plan.

SAMUEL. No. No, that ain't how we runnin' this.

School is your only priority right now —

KEYONNA. Samuel, can you stop.

Missin' one day ain't gon' stop me from goin' to college —

SAMUEL. Yeah I know all that but —

KEYONNA. And you clearly need me.

So just let me help.

> (**SAMUEL** *is silent.*)

Earth to Sam —

SAMUEL. Okay, Keyonna.

> (*A small pause.*)

I honestly don't know how we gon' swing it this time though.

KEYONNA. ...Whatchu mean?

We always swing it.

SAMUEL. ...Lee fired me last night.

KEYONNA. Fired you?

I thought you said he just wanted to talk.

SAMUEL. He did at first. 'Bout some new cleaning supplies.

But halfway through my shift, I saw he was looking at me sideways.

Shift ended, he fired me.

KEYONNA. But why? What happened?

SAMUEL. Apparently somebody been stealin' from the register.

And Lee say he know it's me.

Say I been workin' too hard. Smilin' too much.

KEYONNA. He can't fire you for that.

Not without no proof —

SAMUEL. He already did, Keyonna.

Right in front of everybody.

KEYONNA. ...So you go work at another bar.

One of them fancy joints downtown.

SAMUEL. Lee was doin' me a favor.

No paperwork. Cash in hand every Friday.

Plus all them old heads knew Daddy so wasn't nobody gon' call him out for how young I am.

KEYONNA. Okay, but still.

You gotta work somewhere.

SAMUEL. I know.

I know that.

(A pause.)

KEYONNA. Maybe I can find some last-minute babysittin'?

Chantel's cousin Kanysha still ask me every other week.

SAMUEL. That ain't gon' be enough money.

Plus you know I don't like you hangin' in Ivy City.

KEYONNA. We know half the folks in Ivy City though, Sam.

Chantel go home there every night.

SAMUEL. No, Keyonna.

KEYONNA. Okay. Fine.

I won't ask Kanysha.

But don't expect me to sit this one out, Sam.

If we in a bind, I'm helpin', and ain't nothin' you can do to stop me.

SAMUEL. I could march your ass to the school house —

KEYONNA. You could try.

> *(A pause, but then* **SAMUEL** *smiles.)*

SAMUEL. Why you always gotta be so hardheaded, mo?

KEYONNA. 'Cause I'm me, nigga.

SAMUEL. –

KEYONNA. And because you need me to be.

> *(***KEYONNA*** *pokes* **SAMUEL**. *Or maybe she shoulder-checks him. Something simple and affectionate.)*

SAMUEL. You really think you can dig up some funds today, Key?

On the real?

KEYONNA. On the real.

> *(***KEYONNA*** *reaches into a pocket and retrieves a few dollar bills. She holds them out to* **SAMUEL**.*)*

SAMUEL. Nah. You keep that.

Walk to McDonald's and get you a sausage biscuit or somethin'.

KEYONNA. A sausage biscuit?

Nigga nah. I'm waitin' 'til 10:30 to get me that ninety-nine-cent McChicken.

SAMUEL. Oh yeah?

Get me one too then.

KEYONNA. Boy, I ain't no delivery service.

You want a McChicken, you gotta give me somethin' to sweeten the exchange.

SAMUEL. Sweeten the exchange?

KEYONNA. Chicken ain't free, Sam.

>   (**SAMUEL** *laughs.*)

SAMUEL. Aight. Aight. Let me think.

>   (*He thinks. Then he finds it.*)

>   I got it.

>   You get me that McChicken, I'll let you tell me a story.

KEYONNA. ...Word?

SAMUEL. Just one story, Key.

>   A short one.

>   And I ain't givin' you no damn notes.

KEYONNA. Ain't nobody askin' you for notes —

SAMUEL. You always ask for notes —

KEYONNA. Ain't nobody askin' you for notes!

>   But yes I will obviously tell you a story. Here we go. An oldie but a goodie...

>   (**KEYONNA** *makes a show of preparing this.*
>   **SAMUEL** *rolls his eye.*)

>   (*Putting a hand over his mouth.*) Seamus Reynolds was the son of a fisherman.

>   The poorest fisherman in a village way back in the beginning of time.

>   And I'm talkin' like B.C. or some shit.

>   Before medicine.

>   Before electricity.

>   Before any of our modern comforts.

Back then, lil' Seamus Reynolds only loved two things in this world...

The feeling when a fished tugged on his line.

And his father's smile whenever he reeled one in.

Each time Seamus knew he'd done something good.

For that night, his father would season the fish, grill it to perfection, and feed their entire family.

Just enough bites for everybody to survive another night.

Just enough bites —

SAMUEL. *(Joining in from memory.)* Just enough bites to make his mother smile.

KEYONNA. –

SAMUEL. Just enough bites for shit to be aight.

> *(A pause.* **SAMUEL** *smiles sadly at his sister.)*

Shit used to be simple, Key.

Back when it was just you and Pops on the stoop tellin' y'all lil' story joints.

Me listenin'.

Ma wildin' as usual, but it ain't touch us you know.

Pops had us.

Then one lil' heart attack and boom.

Here we are.

There he went.

> *(***KEYONNA*** *reaches forward and takes* **SAMUEL**'*s hand.)*

KEYONNA. It'll be good again, Sam.

We'll make it happen.

You know that right?

SAMUEL. Yeah.

I know.

> (**SAMUEL** *kisses* **KEYONNA** *atop her head. Then he exits.* **KEYONNA** *watches the door for a few moments, but then she pulls out her phone and dials a number. She waits for a pause. When she gets no answer she leaves a message.)*

KEYONNA. Hey Kanysha,

it's Keyonna.

It's been a minute, but you should hit me up if you need any babysittin' this week.

I gotchu.

And uh... I could honestly use the funds.

So, hit me up.

> (**KEYONNA** *hangs up. As she thinks about what that call might mean, we hear big orchestral space music creeping in.* **KEYONNA** *looks up and smiles. Then* **NATALIE** *appears around a corner. She's dressed as an imperial senator, something simple, elegant, and fit for battle. It should definitely evoke Senator Padmé Amidala in* The Empire Strikes Back. *She crosses to* **KEYONNA** *and offers her a laser sword.)*

Yo where did you even get this —

NATALIE. No time for pleasantries, Anakin.

We must save Obi-Wan.

> (**KEYONNA** *laughs.)*

---

*A license to produce *All the Natalie Portmans* does not include a performance license for any third-party or copyrighted music. Licensees should create an original composition or use music in the public domain. For further information, please see the Music and Third-Party Materials Use Note on page iii.

NATALIE. You saw his distress signal?

> (**KEYONNA** *just looks at* **NATALIE.**)

We're the only ones who can help!

KEYONNA. ...Are we really doing this?

NATALIE. *(Slipping character just slightly.) Yes.*

> (**NATALIE** *offers* **KEYONNA** *the laser sword again. Then* **KEYONNA** *tosses her cell phone and takes it. She looks down at it. And powers it on.)*

KEYONNA. But Padme we can't. I swore to the Jedi Council that I would protect you.

NATALIE. Screw their rules!

Obi-Wan is important to you.

KEYONNA. Obi-Wan is like a father to me.

NATALIE. So we must heed his call!

> (**NATALIE** *hops onto the sofa and starts pressing dials like they're in a spaceship.* **KEYONNA** *hesitates for just a second, but then she jumps onto the sofa too. She powers on her side of the spaceship. They're the perfect team. She looks over at* **NATALIE,** *fully in character now.)*

KEYONNA. It'll be dangerous, Padmé.

NATALIE. Not when we have each other, Annie.

KEYONNA. –

NATALIE. And not when we have the stars!

> *(They fire up their ship as the music swells.)*
>
> *(Then lights fade on two galactic warriors bound for greatness.)*

Scene Four

*(Lights up on a hotel lobby. We don't need to
see much, but we are somewhere spacious and
formal.* **SAMUEL** *leans against something,
waiting. After a pause,* **OVETTA** *enters in
her hotel uniform. She spots her son, takes a
deep breath, and then crosses to him.* **SAMUEL**
stands up a bit straighter.)

OVETTA. Samuel.

There you are.

Give me some sugar.

> *(***OVETTA*** *makes a grab for* **SAMUEL***'s face, but
> he moves out of her reach.)*

Okay.

> *(A pause.)*

You look good.

Handsome. Like your father —

SAMUEL. Where the money at, Ma?

OVETTA. I see.

You been talkin' to your sister.

SAMUEL. Course I have.

OVETTA. She tell you somethin' 'bout me?

'Bout what she think I been up to.

SAMUEL. She ain't had to tell me nothin' 'bout you, Ma.

OVETTA. Exactly. 'Cause you my good boy.

SAMUEL. Nah.

She ain't had to tell me nothin', 'cause I already know
everything there is to know.

OVETTA. –

SAMUEL. You disappear one day, you took an extra shift.

You disappear two days, you fell asleep in the break room and Shalia let you stay.

But you gone three?

You got somethin' to hide, Ma.

OVETTA. It ain't like that, Samuel.

I swear it ain't.

SAMUEL. Then what is it like, hunh?

OVETTA. –

SAMUEL. I'm listenin'.

OVETTA. You know how I used to roll with Millie and them on the weekends?

Millie, and Jocelyn, and Imelda —

SAMUEL. I do.

OVETTA. Well, Millie asked me to roll with her to the casino the other night.

She said it was just gon' be a few hours.

Some slots. Some gossip. Some laughs.

And I said yeah. But I wasn't gon' drink. I was just gon' roll.

Try to be one of the girls again.

Like before —

SAMUEL. But?

OVETTA. But I don't know.

...I lost track of things.

And we was in there so long.

At the bar.

Foolin' with them slots.

Time just went right past me —

SAMUEL. You tellin' me you spent damn near 800 dollars in one night, Ma?

OVETTA. I'm tellin' you I lost control.

Just for a second.

SAMUEL. And whatchu think that second gon' cost me, hunh?

Whatchu think it's gon' cost Keyonna?

Because I can think of a few things.

The electric. The water. The roof over our heads —

OVETTA. I realize that Samuel —

SAMUEL. Do you?

OVETTA. And I am trying to apologize —

SAMUEL. I DON'T WANT YOUR FUCKIN' APOLOGY.

I WANT MY MONEY.

OVETTA. I am at work. Don't you see me at work?

SAMUEL. Keyonna is sixteen.

Sixteen.

She sittin' at home right now with nothin' to eat.

Nobody lookin' out for her.

She don't deserve this, yo.

OVETTA. Keyonna is doin' fine.

Hell, she was doin' wonderful fo' she start coverin' my walls with pictures of white women and talkin' 'bout she a lesbian.

SAMUEL. Don't try to change the subject, aight —

OVETTA. We gotta do somethin' about her, Samuel.

> She don't run round the neighborhood like she used to.

> Ain't got no friends —

SAMUEL. This ain't about Keyonna.

OVETTA. Sure it is.

> It's always about Keyonna.

> 'Cause she just like your father.

> Turn you all the way round tryna make her happy.

> It's like he left this world and she just become him —

SAMUEL. Ma, I swear if you don't cut this bullshit —

OVETTA. It ain't bullshit —

SAMUEL. It is! Everything got to do with you is bullshit.

> Can't you see that?

> "Let me help, Samuel."

> "Let me try."

> "Let me be the momma."

> "I'm ready."

> …

> Only you ain't ready for shit.

> Maybe you never will be.

OVETTA. So that's how you talkin' to me now? Like you a man?

SAMUEL. I am a man.

> 'Cause runnin' behind you made me one.

> Tendin' to Key made me one.

Daddy dyin'?

Just one more reason Sam had to straighten up and run shit.

OVETTA. –

SAMUEL. But I'm so sick of this, yo.

I just wanna go one week with only one thing on my mind.

Just the one good thing I'm workin' at in my life.

And you always gotta make it hard.

OVETTA. You can have your good thing, Sam.

Whatever it is. 'Cause the rent is handled.

Anyway Epps ain't gon' // put nobody out.

SAMUEL. You don't know that though, Ma.

OVETTA. I do actually —

SAMUEL. YOU DON'T —

OVETTA. Come here, Samuel.

SAMUEL. –

OVETTA. Come.

> (**SAMUEL** *let's* **OVETTA** *come to him. She takes his face in her hands.*)

Let me handle it alright?

I can handle it.

SAMUEL. No, you can't, Ma.

Not the way you thinkin'.

OVETTA. It'll just be the one time. For you.

And for Keyonna.

Epps easy.

His needs is simple —

SAMUEL. *No.*

OVETTA. Okay. Okay.

But I can't ask for no more advances.

You know that.

> (**SAMUEL** *removes her hands from his face.*)

I'm sorry —

SAMUEL. Keyonna said you was drunk last night.

That's how you livin'?

OVETTA. I had one drink.

Just the one.

SAMUEL. I gotta go, aight?

OVETTA. Go where?

SAMUEL. Don't worry about it.

OVETTA. Where are you goin', Samuel? —

SAMUEL. To handle your business.

Again.

> (**SAMUEL** *exits.* **OVETTA** *looks after him.*)
>
> (*Lights fade.*)

Scene Five

(The apartment later that afternoon. **KEYONNA** *is in the living room with a* **MAN** *who is carting away the television. She holds the door open for him as he exits.* **CHANTEL** *is also there, clutching her backpack and staying out of the way.)*

KEYONNA. Enjoy it, yo.

That TV been real good to me.

(The **MAN** *nods and exits.* **KEYONNA** *steps away from the open front door and watches him off. Then she pockets the money she just earned and closes the door. She turns to* **CHANTEL** *with an awkward smile.)*

CHANTEL. Sorry. That I just...showed up like this.

KEYONNA. It's fine. Really —

CHANTEL. Like I ain't mean to interrupt your sale or whatever you got goin' on —

KEYONNA. Seriously it's cool, Chantel —

CHANTEL. It's just, I was with Kanysha this mornin'.

KEYONNA. –

CHANTEL. ...When you called her.

She say you was lookin' to babysit?

KEYONNA. Oh.

CHANTEL. Yeah.

KEYONNA. I just...yeah she been askin' so I figured —

CHANTEL. She always askin', Key.

But that don't mean nobody should take her up on it.

Not with them badass kids she got.

KEYONNA. Oh, I figure it would just be the baby.

Since it's a school day or whatever.

CHANTEL. Her kids barely be in school though.

It's like she trainin' 'em up to be dropouts.

KEYONNA. That's fucked up.

CHANTEL. That's Kanysha.

> *(A pause.)*

Anyway.

Uh I saw the call, and I just...

Uh I was on my way to school, and I...

KEYONNA. You what, Chantel? —

CHANTEL. Y'all need money right?

KEYONNA. –

CHANTEL. Like...Ms. O done slipped. And y'all need money?

KEYONNA. Shouldn't you be talkin' to Sam about this?

CHANTEL. Sam ain't got no minutes on his phone.

You know that.

KEYONNA. So you wanna just wait for him?

Talk to him when he get back?

CHANTEL. I'm talkin' to you, Keyonna.

KEYONNA. –

CHANTEL. I'm standin' right here.

Talkin' to you.

KEYONNA. Okay?

CHANTEL. Okay so what's the deal?

Do you need me?

KEYONNA. Do I need you?

CHANTEL. Sorry do y'all need me.

KEYONNA. Ohmygod —

CHANTEL. I'm jus' tryna help, Keyonna.

You are my best friend —

KEYONNA. Am I now?

CHANTEL. Yeah —

KEYONNA. I'm not doin' this, Chantel.

I got too much goin' on and too much to figure out —

CHANTEL. I'm not askin' you to do nothin', okay?

I'm just here to help.

> (**CHANTEL** *fishes into her backpack and pulls out a wad of bills. A pause.*)

KEYONNA. Yoooo.

What?

CHANTEL. I got it to spare.

And if I try to give it to Sam —

KEYONNA. He'll say no.

CHANTEL. Basically. Yeah.

KEYONNA. So why should I say yes?

CHANTEL. Because you know you can, Keyonna.

KEYONNA. –

CHANTEL. Samuel is so sweet.

And he'll bend over backwards for everybody.

But he don't take help.

Even when he know he need it.

KEYONNA. Maybe it's 'cause he don't wanna owe nobody any favors —

CHANTEL. Keyonna, y'all are basically my family.

He ain't gon' owe me.

KEYONNA. But it's Sam.

He gon' feel like he owe you his whole life —

CHANTEL. Then don't tell him.

Just take the money.

And tell him whatever.

I don't know, but don't be stupid, Keyonna.

Don't be proud.

(A small pause.)

KEYONNA. Don't be proud?

CHANTEL. You know what I mean.

KEYONNA. You are somethin' else, Chantel —

CHANTEL. Keyonna don't do this, young —

KEYONNA. You are so fuckin' good at makin' me seem like the bad guy.

Every time.

You are just — why are you like this?

CHANTEL. I don't wanna fight with you —

KEYONNA. YEAH WELL I DON'T WANNA SEE YOU.

(A pause.)

You hear that, best friend?

CHANTEL. –

KEYONNA. I don't want to see you.

(A pause. Then **CHANTEL** *takes the bills, grabs* **KEYONNA***'s hand, and places them in her palm.* **KEYONNA** *accepts the money. Then* **CHANTEL** *heads for the door.)*

So that's it?

I get mad, and you just give up?

No Sam.

So you got no business here?

CHANTEL. I guess so, Key.

KEYONNA. That's perfect. That's...fuck you —

CHANTEL. Hol' up what?

KEYONNA. I said fuck you, Chantel.

CHANTEL. –

KEYONNA. It's bad enough you lie to yourself.

But lyin' to Sam?

That's low.

CHANTEL. I am not lyin' to him.

KEYONNA. So you just lied to me then?

Is that it?

CHANTEL. You know it ain't like that —

KEYONNA. Do I though?

CHANTEL. I don't owe you nothin' Keyonna.

I know shit is hard for you right now but, you ain't gotta —

KEYONNA. YOU KISSED ME CHANTEL.

CHANTEL. –

KEYONNA. You kissed me and then you ran out of here like I stole somethin' from you.

CHANTEL. That ain't exactly how it went down —

KEYONNA. Then after ghostin' me for weeks, you show up right back in my living room —

CHANTEL. Keyonna —

KEYONNA. With my brother.

Holdin' his hand like y'all in the seventh grade.

Barely even lookin' me in my eyes.

CHANTEL. –

KEYONNA. –

CHANTEL. That ain't exactly what happened, Key.

You know it's more complicated than that —

KEYONNA. Just do me a favor, Chan.

Don't come up in here tryna make me out to be the bad friend.

Least I'm honest with my shit.

Least I'm a decent person.

CHANTEL. –

KEYONNA. You waiting for Sam or what?

>   (**CHANTEL** *swallows this. Then she exits the apartment.* **KEYONNA** *takes in her absence, her shoulders falling for a pause, but then lights shift.*)

>   (**NATALIE** *is suddenly there. She's dressed in a simple polka-dot dress, something that evokes her character Novalee Nation from* Where The Heart Is. *She holds a sleeping baby in her arms.* **KEYONNA** *flashes a grateful smile.*)

NATALIE. Well if it ain't the infamous Willy Jack.

You here to abandon me all over again?

(KEYONNA looks at NATALIE with a sad smile but can't find the courage for the game.)

KEYONNA. –

NATALIE. I know you never meant to hurt me all them years ago.

But you did.

You left me in a Walmart.

I was with child —

KEYONNA. I'm sorry.

NATALIE. You sure are sorry.

A sorry son of a bitch.

KEYONNA. –

NATALIE. I ain't takin' you back, Willy Jack.

I ain't givin' up my life for you.

You hear?

(A dramatic pause. NATALIE waits for KEYONNA's next move, but KEYONNA is a bit lost in thought.)

Don't you wanna play?

KEYONNA. I do, but —

NATALIE. Good.

'Cause now's the part when you tell me you never felt the baby's heartbeat.

And I ask why you lied.

And you say sometimes people lie because they don't want things to change.

KEYONNA. I know the plot of *Where The Heart Is* Natalie.

NATALIE. Okay, so let's do it.

I love this stupid movie.

> (**NATALIE** *gets back into position, baby on her hip. She waits for* **KEYONNA** *to begin, but* **KEYONNA** *looks away.* **NATALIE** *takes this in. Then she sets aside her fake baby and crosses to* **KEYONNA**. *She takes her face in her hands.*)

Trust the game, Keyonna.

Trust me.

> (*A breath.*)

I've got you.

I promise.

> (*A smile between them.*)

> (*Lights fade.*)

Scene Six

(Samuel's bedroom. Thirty minutes later.
SAMUEL *and* **CHANTEL** *lie in bed under the
covers. They've just finished having sex, and*
CHANTEL *is enjoying the afterglow.* **SAMUEL**,
however, is a million miles away.)

CHANTEL. Hey, you still with me?

SAMUEL. –

CHANTEL. Sam?

SAMUEL. Sorry.

I'm here. I'm just...

*(***CHANTEL** *sits up, the afterglow gone.)*

CHANTEL. You wanna talk about it?

SAMUEL. This shit just ain't right, Chan.

CHANTEL. I know.

But you already got half of what y'all need, right?

SAMUEL. Yeah, 'cause of Key.

Even though she had to sell her best shit to do it.

CHANTEL. Keyonna would sell the clothes off her back
helpin' you.

You ain't gotta worry about that.

SAMUEL. But it's my job to look out for her.

CHANTEL. And you do look out for her.

Better than any big brother I know.

(A pause. **SAMUEL** *tries to take that in,
but he's too wrapped up in his own head.*
CHANTEL *clocks this.)*

CHANTEL. You know what I remembered the other day?

The first day I met you.

SAMUEL. Oh yeah?

CHANTEL. Yeah it was summer of '99. Or 2000 maybe?

I don't know, but it was at your old house on Hamlin.

I remember I was walkin' by on my way home, just mindin' my own business.

But then I heard you laugh.

One of them belly laughs, you know? Like kids do? Deep from the gut.

So I turned around to see what was good, and it was you and Keyonna.

You had her up on your shoulders so she could catch a lightnin' bug that was tryna get away.

But she kept missin' and she just kept laughin'.

And right as I looked, you reached up and caught it in this lil' plastic cup and Keyonna's whole face just came alive.

She smiled so big.

And you spun her around, and around, and around.

But when you stopped spinnin', y'all was facin' me.

And Keyonna took the cup and she just held it out to me like...*come see, Chantel.*

She ain't even know me.

But she already liked me.

Then Mr. Henry came outside, and he waved me over, and that was basically a wrap.

Only I ain't stay 'cause your father invited me in, Samuel.

I stayed 'cause Keyonna showed me that lightnin' bug like it was meant for me.

Like y'all was meant for me.

SAMUEL. That's a lot of details for you just remembering.

CHANTEL. It's a reason me and Key been tight all these years.

She ain't the only one like a good story.

SAMUEL. Okay, but why are you tellin' me this one?

CHANTEL. 'Cause y'all was workin' together, Samuel.

Like a unit.

And y'all was lovin' each other.

Like I never seen folks love each other.

You know what I mean?

SAMUEL. –

CHANTEL. Y'all gon' get through this.

'Cause you gon' go to Lee, get your pay for the last two weeks, and settle this shit with Epps.

Easy.

Like always —

> (**SAMUEL** *leans in and kisses* **CHANTEL.** *She kisses him back for a moment, granting him this. But then she kisses him on the cheek, stands, and starts getting dressed.*)

SAMUEL. Seriously?

CHANTEL. I got somewhere to be, Samuel.

SAMUEL. We both know you ain't goin' nowhere but home, Chan.

Why not just stay?

CHANTEL. 'Cause.

   I like my house.

   And Tracy'll be lookin' for me.

SAMUEL. Your mother ain't gon' be lookin' for you.

   You used to sleep here every other night.

CHANTEL. But I ain't done that in a while, have I?

SAMUEL. She ain't gon' notice.

   She never notice nothin'.

CHANTEL. Still.

SAMUEL. Whatchu mean "still"? —

CHANTEL. I wanna sleep in my own bed, Sam.

   On my own terms.

> (**CHANTEL** *can't find an article of clothing.*
> *She looks all over for it.*)

SAMUEL. Why you always say stuff like that?

CHANTEL. Stuff like what?

SAMUEL. Like that.

   You think you can't be on your own terms with me?

   Like…you can't be yourself with me?

CHANTEL. That is not what I meant, Samuel.

SAMUEL. Then what did you mean?

CHANTEL. –

SAMUEL. You come here every other day with smashin' on
   your mind, and you say nice shit to me, and you talk to
   me like we family.

   But then you just roll, Chan.

You just peace and act like that shit ain't cruel. But it is.

It's fucked up.

CHANTEL. –

SAMUEL. You can't tell me stories like that, and like make me feel like this, and then just leave.

> (**CHANTEL** *finds the article of clothing but doesn't pull it on.*)

I remember that day in the yard too.

I saw you first.

Out the corner of my eye.

I was showing off.

I wanted you to see me catch that bug.

Would've handed it to you myself, but you know Keyonna.

She always one step ahead.

CHANTEL. –

SAMUEL. Just stay. For a couple more hours.

CHANTEL. You got shit to handle tonight, Samuel.

Real-life shit.

I'll just be in the way —

SAMUEL. When have you ever been in my way?

> (**CHANTEL** *looks at him.*)

Take off those clothes, and get back in this bed, Chantel.

...

Please?

CHANTEL. –

SAMUEL. *Chan.*

CHANTEL. *Okay.*

SAMUEL. –

CHANTEL. Okay.

> (**CHANTEL** *starts peeling off her layers. One by one.* **SAMUEL** *watches her, saying nothing. She climbs back into the bed, and they just lie there, not quite touching. When he's ready,* **SAMUEL** *speaks.*)

SAMUEL. I love you.

> (**CHANTEL** *looks away from him.*)

I don't expect you to say it back.

But I do.

And I wanted you to know.

> (*Lights fade.*)

Scene Seven

*(NATALIE smiles and exits just as the front
door opens. It's OVETTA. She pauses in the
doorway and peers around. Maybe she can't
quite see where she's going. She is very drunk.)*

OVETTA. Henry Ray?

Henry Ray is you in this house?

If so, you better come on out here and get you some of
this.

Ain't in the best condition, but it's yours!

I'm yours!

(She enters the apartment.)

Henry Ray?

KEYONNA. He ain't here, Ma.

*(She stands. She crosses to her mother and
closes the front door.)*

You want some water?

OVETTA. I want your daddy to come home —

KEYONNA. Or a lie down? —

OVETTA. Lee keep him at that bar too late.

Ain't that many folks need a burger this time a night —

KEYONNA. Okay. I know, Ma.

But maybe if you lay down for a minute —

*(KEYONNA grabs for her mother's arm, but
OVETTA evades her.)*

OVETTA. Don't you put your hands on me.

I'm a grown woman.

I made you.

I can break you if I want.

> *(She leans in, drunk.)*

You want me to break you?

KEYONNA. Fuck this noise.

> *(She crosses to Samuel's bedroom door. She knocks.)*

Sam?

Sam, I need you.

OVETTA. Henry Ray!

I want some sugar in this bowl.

You hear me?

KEYONNA. Samuel!

> *(The bedroom door opens, but it's **CHANTEL**.)*

Where is he?

CHANTEL. He talkin' to Lee remember?

KEYONNA. Great. That's helpful.

OVETTA. Henry Ray, I know.

I know I done you wrong.

KEYONNA. Fuck.

Can you just help me then?

> *(**CHANTEL** enters the living room, and they both approach **OVETTA**.)*

OVETTA. It's just...these kids. They cost too much.

I love 'em. I do.

But the cost.

Nobody tell you 'bout the cost.

KEYONNA. Ma.

I'ma need you to calm // down now.

> *(They lift* **OVETTA** *up by her arms and attempt moving her to the sofa, but she resists violently, knocking* **KEYONNA** *back. This stops all three women.)*

CHANTEL. Ms. O. It's okay. You okay —

OVETTA. I ain't been a good mother to you, Keyonna.

I know that.

But I try.

I'm tryin'.

You know that, right?

You see it?

> *(***OVETTA** *keeps her eyes on her daughter.* **CHANTEL** *looks from* **KEYONNA** *to* **OVETTA** *and back. Then she takes charge.)*

CHANTEL. Yeah.

She see it.

> *(***CHANTEL** *lifts the older woman and carts her to the sofa.)*

OVETTA. Reach in my pocket won't you?

> *(***CHANTEL** *reaches into* **OVETTA***'s jean pockets. Maybe she searches both pockets before she finds it, but when she does, she produces a wad of bills.* **KEYONNA** *and* **CHANTEL** *just stare at it.)*

OVETTA. Is that enough, babygirl?

It should be enough to get y'all through.

> (**OVETTA** *loosens her grip and sinks into the pillow cushions. After a pause, she is fast asleep.* **CHANTEL** *stands. She pulls a blanket over the sleeping woman. Then she turns to* **KEYONNA.**)

KEYONNA. How much money is that?

> (**CHANTEL** *counts.*)

CHANTEL. Four hundred dollars.

KEYONNA. Where the hell did she get it?

CHANTEL. That don't matter.

It's what y'all need right?

> (**KEYONNA** *takes the money. She counts it.*)

KEYONNA. I was so mean to her last night.

She said some messed-up shit to me.

And I said more shit back.

And she just...

She always make it so hard to stay mad.

CHANTEL. She a drunk, Key.

KEYONNA. But I raised my voice.

I got all up in her face.

CHANTEL. Was she pokin' at you though?

KEYONNA. Yeah but —

CHANTEL. What I always say, Keyonna?

KEYONNA. –

CHANTEL. What I say?

KEYONNA. Morning wash away the night.

CHANTEL. Exactly.

She ain't gon' remember that.

You just fine.

You good.

(**KEYONNA** *exhales.*)

KEYONNA. I miss you, Chantel.

CHANTEL. ...I know.

KEYONNA. Don't you miss me?

CHANTEL. It ain't that simple, Keyonna —

KEYONNA. But it used to be.

Before.

CHANTEL. ...I'm not strong like you.

KEYONNA. But you are.

You are strong —

CHANTEL. I'm not.

I'm really not. —

KEYONNA. Okay. Just.

...Imagine for one second that everything was different.

My dad never passed.

Shit never got so intense for me.

I never rushed it, you know?

I just waited for you.

I just waited until you was ready.

CHANTEL. –

KEYONNA. How 'bout then?

Then would you be strong?

> (**CHANTEL** *thinks about this. Maybe she's even letting a very small window crack open inside. But then there's a heavy knock at the door.)*

OVETTA. *(Still asleep.)* Henry Ray?

> *(The knock sounds again and both girls let this moment go.)*

KEYONNA. Who is it?

EPPS. *(Offstage.)* It's Epps.

KEYONNA. We'll have your money tomorrow, Mr. Epps. I promise.

Ain't no need for you to be knockin' this late at night.

EPPS. *(Offstage.)* It ain't about that.

> (**KEYONNA** *and* **CHANTEL** *exchange a look.)*

KEYONNA. Then what is it about?

EPPS. *(Offstage.)* Just open up the door, Keyonna —

KEYONNA. Not without a good reason —

EPPS. *(Offstage.)* It's about your brother, goddammit.

Lee just called me.

KEYONNA & CHANTEL. –

EPPS. *(Offstage.)* Hello?

I said Lee just called me.

From the bar?

Some shit went down.

(Another knock. **NATALIE** *appears at the edge of the stage. She watches.)*

CHANTEL. Keyonna?

KEYONNA. –

CHANTEL. Keyonna, I think we should open it.

*(***KEYONNA*** *takes a deep breath. Then she looks to the door. As she makes a decision...)*

(Blackout.)

ACT II

Scene One

(In darkness, we hear the settling of two chairs. Then lights come up on the visiting room of the New Beginnings Youth Development Center. It's three weeks later. **SAMUEL** *sits in a chair at a table, very anxious.* **KEYONNA** *sits across from him, taking him in. He's* **SAMUEL** *for sure. He's her brother. But there's something different about him. Something manic.)*

KEYONNA. Sorry I'm late.

SAMUEL. It's cool. You here, right?

I mean... I was startin' to think you wasn't gon' come.

KEYONNA. Why would I not come visit you?

SAMUEL. I'on know.

...I guess I just figured maybe you still mad at me?

Maybe you need some time to not hate me.

You know.

KEYONNA. Hate ain't somethin' we do, Sam.

(A small pause.)

SAMUEL. How's Ma?

She doin', aight?

KEYONNA. Not really.

SAMUEL. Whatchu mean not really?

> She still workin' right?

> She still helpin' you —

KEYONNA. Course she still workin'.

> That ain't what I meant.

SAMUEL. Then what's wrong with her?

KEYONNA. I don't know.

> Maybe she feel guilty?

> Seem like every time I turn around she there.

> Askin' me what I need.

> Where I been.

> If I'm hungry —

SAMUEL. Well, that's good right?

> That's like...normal mother shit.

KEYONNA. No, it's annoyin', it's desperate, and it's late.

SAMUEL. Key come on —

KEYONNA. It is, Sam.

> Maybe if she tried all this shit earlier we wouldn't be in this situation —

SAMUEL. Don't do that, aight.

> What happened to me, ain't on Ma.

KEYONNA. Oh, it's not?

SAMUEL. No.

> I'm the one got hemmed up.

KEYONNA. Whatever.

SAMUEL. Not whatever.

> Truth.

KEYONNA. WHATEVER.

> *(A pause.)*

SAMUEL. How's Epps?

KEYONNA. Fine for now.

Long as we got rent on the first.

SAMUEL. And you got a plan for that right?

KEYONNA. I'm lookin' for a job, yeah.

Figure if I can make some pennies, we'll at least have enough to cover him.

Ain't enough for food though.

So Ma gon' have to work somethin' out with the hotel manager.

I told her that.

SAMUEL. She can't be borrowin' from the kitchen again, Key.

That shit don't look good.

If she get caught —

KEYONNA. What other choice we got, Sam?

It's that or go hungry.

SAMUEL. Still —

KEYONNA. Look I gotta make this work the only way I know how, aight.

Just...let it be.

> *(A pause.)*

SAMUEL. I fucked up, Key.

KEYONNA. Yeah okay.

SAMUEL. Nah. For real.

You out there on your own.

You ain't got no money.

No help.

Fuck was I thinkin'? —

KEYONNA. You wasn't thinkin'.

SAMUEL. –

KEYONNA. I mean you was tryin'.

But you can't think with just you, Sam.

It's gotta be both of us.

You can't just up and decide you gon' fix shit.

SAMUEL. I was just doin' my job, aight?

I was bein' the big brother —

KEYONNA. Are you serious right now?

SAMUEL. Yeah.

KEYONNA. Threatnin' Lee was not you bein' a big brother.

You was just supposed to talk to him —

SAMUEL. Ain't nobody threaten Lee.

Is that what he sayin'?

I threatened him?

KEYONNA. That's what everybody sayin'.

SAMUEL. Everybody like who?

KEYONNA. Everybody like everybody —

SAMUEL. Look I ain't threaten him, aight?

I mighta raised my voice a lil' bit.

'Cause of the way he was talkin' to me.

But I ain't threaten him.

KEYONNA. Raised your voice about what though?

You can't ask for help and disrespect somebody at the same time.

SAMUEL. You wasn't there, Key.

You ain't hear what he was sayin'.

KEYONNA. It couldn'ta been that bad, Sam.

They was just words —

SAMUEL. That bar mean somethin' to me.

KEYONNA. –

SAMUEL. And Lee ain't had no right to talk to me like that.

Not there.

Not ever.

> *(A pause.)*

KEYONNA. What did he say to you?

SAMUEL. It don't matter.

KEYONNA. Sam —

SAMUEL. They was just words, right?

KEYONNA. *Sam.*

SAMUEL. –

KEYONNA. Was it about Daddy?

SAMUEL. He ain't had no right bringin' him up, you know?

'Cause Lee's is my spot.

Lee's was Daddy's spot.

I was just sittin' there on a stool, sneakin' me a sip, when this thought just hit me.

This shit ain't right.

This is my place.

This where I'm me.

And Lee...he oughta know that.

He oughta help me.

KEYONNA. –

SAMUEL. Instead he firin' me, and givin' me shit when he know what I been through.

He mean muggin' me in front the whole bar.

Whisperin' shit.

KEYONNA. –

SAMUEL. And before I knew it, I just stood up.

I looked him straight in his eyes, and I said,

"My sister need me, Lee.

You know she do, and you know why.

So don't fire me.

Help me, dawg.

Cut all this bullshit and just help."

KEYONNA. –

SAMUEL. But that motherfucker just smiled.

He smiled at me and he said,

"You ain't your father, Samuel.

I don't owe you shit."

KEYONNA. –

SAMUEL. And I don't know, Key, I just...

I hopped right over the bar and I went at him.

Time I come to, Lee was on the floor and I was on top of him.

I hit him so many times one of his eyes ain't even look like an eye no more.

Just look like a pocket of blood.

Just look mangled.

Took two niggas to pull me off.

And when Lee finally get to his feet, he ain't say nothin' to me.

He just picked up the phone and call the cops.

So...I just waited.

I figure I run, that'd be worse.

> (*A long pause.*)

KEYONNA. Least you ain't kill him.

> (**SAMUEL** *chuckles.*)

SAMUEL. That's what you got out of all of that?

Least I ain't kill him?

KEYONNA. Yeah.

I would have.

SAMUEL. You really would've though.

> (*They both chuckle, but* **SAMUEL** *is very near breaking down.*)

...I'm sorry, Key.

KEYONNA. I know.

> (*A pause.*)

But it's just ninety days, right?

SAMUEL. Plus a year of probation.

KEYONNA. That ain't nothin'.

That's a win.

SAMUEL. It ain't.

I hate it in here, Key.

They talk to us like we all broken furniture or some shit.

Got me goin' to therapy.

Askin' 'bout you. Askin' 'bout Ma.

KEYONNA. That's what happen at youth centers, Sam.

Rehabilitation —

SAMUEL. Yeah, well I ain't like these dudes in here, aight?

I'm good.

I'm solid, you know?

KEYONNA. I know.

> *(A small pause.)*

SAMUEL. Yo, you heard from Chantel at all?

> *(**KEYONNA** sits up a bit straighter.)*

I been callin' her.

Want her to come see me.

But she ain't been pickin' up —

KEYONNA. I ain't seen Chantel in weeks.

SAMUEL. Weeks? Whatchu mean?

She know I'm in here, right?

You told her I'm in here?

KEYONNA. She know.

> *(Before **SAMUEL** can push back, there's the ding of an overhead bell.)*

VOICE OVER INTERCOM. Attention all visitors, this is your five-minute warning. I repeat, visiting hours will be up in five minutes.

SAMUEL. Shit. That's your cue right?

KEYONNA. Yeah, I gotta go now if I'm gon' get the bus.

SAMUEL. Can't you wait for the next one?

KEYONNA. Next one don't come for forty minutes, Sam.

SAMUEL. Right.

Metro ain't shit as usual.

(A small pause.)

KEYONNA. I'll be back next week though.

And I'll bring you some CDs.

SAMUEL. You promise?

*(**KEYONNA** reaches forward and takes his hand.)*

KEYONNA. I promise, Samuel.

*(**SAMUEL** looks down at her hand. He needed that touch.)*

It's just ninety days.

Just them ninety and it's you and me again.

It's us.

(A breath.)

(Lights out.)

Scene Two

(Lights come up in full on the house. It's different, cleaner somehow. And there's no evidence that Keyonna still sleeps in the living room. **NATALIE** *stands center stage dressed like a Civil War wife; think flowing curls, a sad damsel if we've ever seen one. It definitely evokes her character Sara from* Cold Mountain. *The front door opens.* **KEYONNA** *enters, holding grocery bags, but she stops in the doorway once she sees* **NATALIE**.*)*

NATALIE. *(Southern accent.)* Hello there, soldier.

I'm a lonely widow raising my baby all alone.

I can't offer you much besides a warm bed, but it's yours.

If you want it —

KEYONNA. Not now, Nat.

NATALIE. Awww, but I worked so hard on this one.

Look at this getup.

KEYONNA. I know. I wish I could, but I've gotta —

NATALIE. The dutiful soldier can't leave the battlefield.

I get it.

KEYONNA. I'm sorry.

NATALIE. Don't be.

KEYONNA. –

NATALIE. I'll be right here when you're ready.

(Footsteps sound behind **KEYONNA**.*)*

OVETTA. *(Offstage.)* You goin' in or what, Keyonna?

(**NATALIE** *frowns and exits.*)

KEYONNA. Shit. Sorry.

(**KEYONNA** *fully enters the apartment, followed by* **OVETTA**, *who also carries grocery bags. They cross into the kitchen, and* **KEYONNA** *begins removing items from the bags. They are an assortment of sealed, unmarked containers, some canned goods, and some dry goods.* **OVETTA** *starts putting the items away, just as* **KEYONNA** *pulls out her phone and looks at the screen.*)

OVETTA. ...That's the third time you done looked at that phone in ten minutes.

You expectin' somebody important?

KEYONNA. Nah. Just...checkin' the time.

OVETTA. You sure?

KEYONNA. ...Sure about what?

OVETTA. I pay attention, you know. I clock everything.

Might only have two kids, but that child always made it feel like three.

(**KEYONNA** *unpacks the groceries.*)

You miss her. You call her.

That's what friends do.

KEYONNA. We ain't friends no more.

OVETTA. Child please.

That right there is a tie that bind.

KEYONNA. Can we *not*, Ma.

(*A small pause, but then* **OVETTA** *reaches.*)

OVETTA. You can talk to me, you know.

You can...rely on me —

KEYONNA. *(Not ready.)* Did you remember to get the eggs? I'on see 'em.

> *(***OVETTA*** *pauses, hands* ***KEYONNA*** *the eggs. They continue with the groceries for a moment.)*

OVETTA. I been talkin' to Shalia 'bout givin' me some extra shifts.

See if I can't get some more money in my next check.

KEYONNA. You think she'll say yes?

OVETTA. Probably not.

I ain't the most trustworthy employee.

KEYONNA. Then why even bring it up, Ma?

OVETTA. Because.

We gotta communicate you and me.

Otherwise come the first, Epps be right back at that door cussin' up a storm.

> *(***KEYONNA*** *shrugs and continues her work.)*

You had any luck lookin'?

KEYONNA. I got an interview at Safeway tomorrow.

They fired two cashiers last week, so I feel like they actually gon' hire me.

OVETTA. Well, that's good.

That's somethin'!

KEYONNA. Yeah.

> *(***OVETTA*** *pauses with the groceries, eyeing her daughter.)*

OVETTA. Keyonna that's good news you just told me.

You know that right?

KEYONNA. I do.

OVETTA. So, act like it.

KEYONNA. Act like what, Ma?

OVETTA. Act like this house still got some light left in it.

Like you still my ass-backwards daughter, more interested in a copy of *Vanity Fair* than the real world.

Like you *you.*

> (**KEYONNA** *is unmoved.*)

We still gotta try to be us, Keyonna.

Even without Samuel —

KEYONNA. I am bein' me, Ma.

OVETTA. This ain't you.

My daughter might be a whole lotta headache, but she ain't like this.

She light up a room. Not suck it dry.

KEYONNA. Can you please stop talkin' about me like we two besties.

I'm Keyonna. You Ovetta.

I do my thing. You do whatever yours is.

OVETTA. So, you just don't want to conversate at all?

You just wanna be strangers under one roof.

KEYONNA. I *want* you to just back up off me, Ma.

For real.

> (**KEYONNA** *unpacks groceries for a moment,*
> *but* **OVETTA** *just watches her.*)

OVETTA. You ain't gotta be surly with me.

I'm tryin' here.

KEYONNA. Yeah well, I'm tired so —

OVETTA. And tired equal rude to you?

That's how you livin' nowadays?

KEYONNA. I ain't livin' no kind of way, aight?

I'm just tryna put these groceries away in peace —

OVETTA. Ain't nobody stoppin' your peace —

KEYONNA. You are, Ma.

You steppin' all up in it even though I'm askin' you to stop.

OVETTA. That's 'cause you ain't askin' politely.

KEYONNA. Okay.

Either be quiet or please go to your room.

OVETTA. ...My room?

KEYONNA. –

OVETTA. You think you can just boss me like that?

After all I done for you —

KEYONNA. YOU AIN'T DONE NOTHIN' FOR ME, OVETTA.

...Not a thing.

OVETTA. –

KEYONNA. Now do you think you can handle keepin' quiet, or do I need to put on headphones to drown you out?

(A pause.)

OVETTA. I think we need to back this conversation up a few steps —

KEYONNA. Yeah okay. Let's do that —

OVETTA. I am the momma in this house, Keyonna.

Me.

Not you. Not Samuel. Not nobody else.

Me.

KEYONNA. Since when?

OVETTA. Since forever!

Since I wiped your shitty ass for three whole years, and washed your face, and put clothes on your back, and food in your stomach —

KEYONNA. Since when?

OVETTA. Since I carried you!

Since I kissed you atop your head when you was fallin' asleep.

And since I sang to you. All the hymns I used to sing to you —

KEYONNA. I don't remember that —

OVETTA. Since I loved you.

That's since when. That's the only since I know.

Since I loved you.

Ain't that enough for you to show me some respect around here.

To talk to me like I'm somebody.

Like I matter to you —

KEYONNA. SAMUEL IS GONE, MA.

OVETTA. –

KEYONNA. He sittin' in that place all by himself.

And you want me to feel sorry for you?

OVETTA. I want you to respect me.

KEYONNA. Yeah well, I can't.

I can't respect you. And I can barely respect myself.

So, unless you got some other need you want me to fill, I just wanna focus on these groceries.

> (*A pause.* **KEYONNA** *returns to the groceries, but* **OVETTA** *is very still. Her eyes never leave her daughter.*)

OVETTA. Drinkin' ain't easy you know.

I mean liftin' the bottle, suckin' it dry, that part is definitely easy.

But it's when you set the bottle down.

And you know what it mean.

What it weigh.

That part break you up every time.

It's like I'm still me. Sort of.

But I'm also still all these lil' pieces all over the damn floor.

And I know that ain't what a momma is supposed to be Keyonna.

I know it.

But that's what I am.

That's who I am.

And broken up and all, I still would like to be loved by you.

To be needed by somebody.

To help with the damn groceries —

> (**KEYONNA** *pulls headphones from her pockets, interrupting her mother. She puts*

them in, and turns on her CD player. This should take a few moments, but **OVETTA** *watches every second of it. She cracks open before us. Eventually, the low hum of pop music fills the room,* and **KEYONNA** *continues with the groceries. After a very long pause,* **OVETTA** *goes to a low cabinet, removes a fifth of whiskey, and walks into her bedroom. She shuts the door.* **KEYONNA** *nods along to the music.)*

---

*A license to produce *All the Natalie Portmans* does not include a performance license for any third-party or copyrighted music. Licensees should create an original composition or use music in the public domain. For further information, please see the Music and Third-Party Materials Use Note on page iii.

Scene Three

(A week later. The living room is dark. **KEYONNA** *enters from her bedroom [formerly Samuel's bedroom]. She's in the process of changing out of her cashier's uniform into the costume of a '90s teenager; think faded jeans, big t-shirt, baseball cap, real tomboy aesthetic. It's really working, but there's a problem: she's being trailed by* **NATALIE***, who's dressed in the same costume.)*

KEYONNA. Oh, come on! It's a good movie!

NATALIE. I'm very aware of that. I was the star, remember?

KEYONNA. Then how come you don't wanna do it?

NATALIE. I do want to.

I do.

It's just —

KEYONNA. Besides, you always play the good parts.

I wanna be Ann this time.

I like all her lil' baseball caps.

> *(***NATALIE*** just looks at* **KEYONNA***.* **KEYONNA** *looks back.)*

It's just a part, Nat.

NATALIE. It's my part.

KEYONNA. *Wow.* Okay.

NATALIE. It is.

I play Ann, the daughter.

Suzie Sarandon played Adele, the mom.

KEYONNA. So, you get to be a teenager and I gotta be Susan Sarandon?

NATALIE. Oh, please.

Everybody wants to be Susan Sarandon.

KEYONNA. Not me. I wanna be Ann.

(She adjusts her cap, feeling herself.)

Adele is crazy anyways.

NATALIE. Adele is not crazy.

She loves Ann.

She just forgets that sometimes.

Do you even remember the movie, Keyonna?

KEYONNA. Yes, I do Natalie.

It's depressing as fuck, but Ann's fits are nice.

NATALIE. It is not depressing. It's complicated.

KEYONNA. Complicated then.

Whatever. Can we just do this before I'm too tired.

(A pause as **KEYONNA** *gets into character. She mopes, the perfect, angry white teen. But* **NATALIE** *won't engage.)*

...What, Nat?

NATALIE. I don't understand what's happening.

You said, "Let's do *Anywhere But Here*." I said, "Ohmygod yes."

And now, I don't know...you're like demanding things.

KEYONNA. I don't remember demanding anything from you.

NATALIE. You're like...exhausted all the time now.

And you don't play right.

You don't play the same.

> *(A pause.)*

KEYONNA. How is it exactly that you want me to play, Nat?

NATALIE. I don't know.

Like you like it?

Like you like me?

Just...like before everything was terrible.

> *(That hangs. **KEYONNA** removes the cap. Game over.)*

Keyonna, no.

Let's just play.

I'm sorry. I'm sorry.

I made it not fun.

KEYONNA. It's cool, Nat.

I'm hungry anyways.

> *(**KEYONNA** goes into the kitchen. Eats from a can of green beans. **NATALIE** watches her for a few beats, unsure how she fits into a moment like this. Then, she has an idea.)*

NATALIE. How about a story? You could tell me one?

> *(A very small pause.)*

KEYONNA. ...What?

NATALIE. A story! I hear you telling them all the time.

About fishermen, and houses that grow feet, and boys with heads the size of balloons.

KEYONNA. –

NATALIE. Ooooo! Or you could write one.

  We've never done that before.

  I'll be your test audience.

  Tell you what's what.

  Like Samuel does.

  Just like that.

  It'll be fun —

KEYONNA. No, thanks.

NATALIE. Oh, come on, Keyonna.

  Just one story!

  For me.

KEYONNA. *(Suddenly tense.)* Yo, could you maybe not be all over me right now?

NATALIE. I am not all over you —

KEYONNA. You are actually. You ain't stopped talkin' at me since I got home.

  And it's like that every day.

  I walk in here and you're just like...*present*.

NATALIE. I'm...not.

  I'm just here, Keyonna.

  I just want to spend time with you.

KEYONNA. Yeah well, I'm tired, Natalie.

  I worked today.

  Have you ever heard of work?

  Have you ever had a real job?

      (A pause.)

NATALIE. ...What is that supposed to mean?

KEYONNA. Nothing.

Fuck.

Just leave me alone.

> (**KEYONNA** *goes to her dream board, starts refining it.* **NATALIE** *watches for a moment, dumbstruck. But then she's angry. She goes to* **KEYONNA***. She positions her body between the teenager and the dream board.*)

Natalie.

Move.

NATALIE. No.

I won't.

KEYONNA. And why is that?

NATALIE. Because this is not what we do.

We have fun.

KEYONNA. Get out of my way, Nat.

NATALIE. *No.*

KEYONNA. –

NATALIE. Not until you do something — anything — besides moping around this apartment.

Be more like Ann.

She grabbed for what she wanted.

She went to Brown. You could go to Brown —

KEYONNA. Can we please stop talking about that stupid fucking movie?

I've moved on.

NATALIE. It is not stupid! It's a fantastic film! I'm very proud of it!

You yourself have watched it multiple times —

KEYONNA. *Natalie* —

NATALIE. You have!

You love *Anywhere But Here*!

It's a good story, Nat.

That's what you always say.

And I trust you because you're the storyteller, Keyonna.

You know things.

You believe in things —

KEYONNA. I don't —

NATALIE. You do. You definitely do —

KEYONNA. WILL YOU PLEASE JUST SHUT THE FUCK UP!

> *(A small pause.* **NATALIE** *is shocked, but* **KEYONNA** *isn't done.)*

Okay, you want a story, Nat?

I'll give you a story.

A story and a fantastic film all wrapped up in one.

Let's see. Here we go.

It's 2009 in the nation's capital, and there's a girl, a teenager, let's call her Keyonna.

She's got the kinda dreams that her little old city can't handle, but that's never stopped her — never even phased her.

'Cause she's gonna get out.

She's gonna make it.

She's gonna go to film school out west, and make a buncha cool-ass friends in LA, and write the best motherfucking screenplays the world has ever read, and make the most badass movies the world has ever seen, and have the best friends and the best life and eat the best foods and live happily ever after —

NATALIE. Keyonna this is not what I meant —

KEYONNA. And kiss girls.

Pretty girls.

And live in big houses with bomb-ass swimming pools filled to the brim with strung-out movie stars who can't stay away from her —

NATALIE. *Hey* —

KEYONNA. Only some nights.

Not every night, but some nights.

She'll wake up, she'll wander that big-ass mansion and touch its walls, and wonder... Who am I? That I think I deserve any of this?

That I think I get to have this?

The queen of fucking France or some shit?

An empress?

Fucking Meryl Streep?

NATALIE. –

KEYONNA. I am none of those things, Natalie.

NATALIE. But you can be.

You can —

KEYONNA. I can't —

NATALIE. I don't believe that —

KEYONNA. Natalie —

> (**NATALIE** *crosses the room and kisses* **KEYONNA**. *It stuns them both, a sudden and electric choice. But then it ends. They just look at each other.)*

Why did you do that?

NATALIE. I don't know.

You were sad.

KEYONNA. I didn't want you to do that.

NATALIE. Didn't you, though?

KEYONNA. –

NATALIE. Isn't that...

KEYONNA. –

NATALIE. Isn't this...

> *(A pause.)*

I'm sorry —

KEYONNA. Can you just go?

NATALIE. *What?*

KEYONNA. I need you to go, Nat.

NATALIE. But I want to be here.

I want to help you.

KEYONNA. Please, just go.

> (**NATALIE** *goes quiet. She tries to catch* **KEYONNA**'s *eyes, but* **KEYONNA** *won't look at her. After a few moments,* **NATALIE** *exits.* **KEYONNA** *exhales.)*
>
> *(Lights.)*

Scene Four

(Lights up on the visiting room of the New Beginnings Youth Development Center. **SAMUEL** *sits in a chair across from* **CHANTEL**. *Her hands are clasped in her lap.)*

SAMUEL. Seriously?

Three weeks in here and you just showin' up?

CHANTEL. I was busy, Samuel.

SAMUEL. Busy with what?

CHANTEL. Shit got crazy at home.

Uh...Tracy got caught shopliftin' in Maryland and they picked her up.

We had to deal with her bail, plus you know she got priors. It was a whole thing.

SAMUEL. Ain't it always a whole thing though, Chan?

CHANTEL. –

SAMUEL. That's how we live.

Crazy shit happen.

Every day.

But we still find a way to show up for each other.

CHANTEL. –

SAMUEL. Keyonna say you ain't been stoppin' by the house.

Say you just ghosted.

CHANTEL. –

SAMUEL. You wanna explain that shit to me.

CHANTEL. Keyonna and me been on pause for a minute now, Sam.

You been knew that.

SAMUEL. I know y'all wasn't talkin' but I also know that when push come to shove, all that petty shit gotta be out.

I know that if I'm in here, Keyonna need you out there.

CHANTEL. It's complicated, Sam.

That's what I'm tryna tell you.

That's why I'm here.

SAMUEL. Then say it.

If you here to explain yourself, then do it.

CHANTEL. I am not here to explain myself.

I don't have to explain myself to nobody.

SAMUEL. Yo, you are wildin' right now.

We were datin', Chan.

I know you ain't wanna call it that.

But the last person I talked to before I messed up was you.

You was holdin' me down.

CHANTEL. I know.

But Sam that ain't our issue right now.

SAMUEL. Oh it's not?

CHANTEL. No.

Our issue is Keyonna.

(A pause.)

SAMUEL. Okay. What's the deal?

CHANTEL. She ain't been in school in two weeks.

And she was in and out before that.

I thought you should know.

SAMUEL. She skip shit sometimes.

But she always stay on top of her work.

CHANTEL. This ain't like before.

She ain't showin' up for tests.

She ain't charmin' no teachers.

She just...absent.

SAMUEL. –

CHANTEL. She's failin' out, Sam.

(They let that hang in the air.)

SAMUEL. You stop by the house?

Check on her?

CHANTEL. I stopped by the hotel.

Talked to Ms. O.

She say Keyonna workin' evenings.

Got herself a cashier job.

But it also seem like Ms. O don't know about the school stuff.

SAMUEL. Did you tell her?

CHANTEL. I did.

But...

SAMUEL. But what, Chantel?

CHANTEL. She ain't look too good herself, Sam.

She was movin' slow.

Like just talkin' to me was work.

SAMUEL. She in that sauce again.

CHANTEL. Deep in it.

SAMUEL. Then you gotta go by the house.

You gotta check on Key.

CHANTEL. That's actually what we need to talk about.

SAMUEL. –

CHANTEL. I can't go check on her.

SAMUEL. Whatchu mean you can't?

CHANTEL. I mean you need to send somebody else.

SAMUEL. Somebody else like who?

CHANTEL. Somebody like one of your boys.

Or like Epps.

Can you try him?

SAMUEL. Epps don't give a shit about us.

You know that.

CHANTEL. But he can still just have a few words with her.

Make sure she straight.

SAMUEL. Nah, you talkin' crazy, Chan.

You gotta do it,

It's gotta be you.

CHANTEL. It can't be me —

SAMUEL. Why not though? —

CHANTEL. *(Firm.)* Because I'll just make it worse, Sam.

I'll just make whatever is goin' on worse.

(A pause.)

SAMUEL. Look.

I know girls fight and all,

But this is my sister we talkin' about, Chan.

You love Keyonna.

More than anything.

Hell, you love her more than me half the damn time —

CHANTEL. Yeah, Sam.

...

I do.

> *(A pause.)*

And what I'm tellin' you, is that you need to send somebody over there who ain't me.

> *(Another pause.* **SAMUEL** *sits back in his chair. He's doing mental math. He's taking this in.)*

SAMUEL. Yoooo.

You are...you are somethin' else, Chantel.

CHANTEL. I'm not.

I'm just me.

SAMUEL. You a liar.

You been lyin' to me.

CHANTEL. I know. I know but —

SAMUEL. And Keyonna just...she just...

Fuck did somethin' happen between y'all?

CHANTEL. –

SAMUEL. Did it?

CHANTEL. We kissed.

Once.

SAMUEL. –

CHANTEL. A lil' bit after your father passed.

SAMUEL. ...And then y'all just stopped bein' cool?

CHANTEL. I was scared, Sam.

SAMUEL. You don't get scared, Chantel.

Whole time I been knowin' you, I ain't never seen you scared.

CHANTEL. Maybe that's 'cause you ain't never scared me.

SAMUEL. Yo, what the fuck is that supposed to mean?

CHANTEL. Nothin'. Sorry that came out wrong.

SAMUEL. Damn straight it came out wrong.

CHANTEL. I'm sorry. I'm just.

I am SO sorry.

(A pause. As long as they need.)

SAMUEL. I think you should go, Chan.

CHANTEL. –

SAMUEL. I think you should take your shit and get up out of here.

*(**CHANTEL** starts to gather her things.)*

But one more thing before you do.

*(**CHANTEL** pauses.)*

My sister is good people.

She the best kind of people.

CHANTEL. Don't you think I know that?

SAMUEL. Then you should act like it, Chan.

CHANTEL. –

SAMUEL. You should act like it, or you should stay in your corner of Northeast.

Leave ours be.

(Lights fade.)

Scene Five

(The apartment. The lights are low. And **KEYONNA** *sits on her sofa. She's in her work uniform, but she holds a pen and paper. She writes furiously. After a few moments, she pauses and looks up from her work. She eats a few bites of green beans from a can. Then she returns to the work.)*

(After a beat, there's the loud banging of a door outside. Then we hear heavy footsteps. Then the front door of the apartment bangs open. **OVETTA** *stumbles in. She's drunk, half-dressed, and nearly falls over but manages to catch herself just as her purse comes flying in through the front door. It's been hurled inside by someone.)*

OVETTA. *(Yelling out the door.)* Fuck you nigga!

You ain't shit!

And your limp dick ain't shit neither!

EPPS. *(Offstage.)* I want y'all out.

You hear me?

I want y'all gone.

OVETTA. You ain't kickin' me out.

Not much as you smile at me from that porch.

Shakin' that fifth in my face.

Beckoning me.

Beggin' me —

EPPS. *(Offstage.)* Just get your shit and go, Ovetta!

I'm done! —

OVETTA. Eat my ass! —

EPPS. *(Offstage.)* I'm done!

> (**KEYONNA** *crosses to the door and pulls* **OVETTA** *back into the apartment. She steps onto the porch.)*

KEYONNA. Mr. Epps.

Hold up.

I said hold up.

EPPS. *(Offstage.)* I mean it, Keyonna.

I want y'all gone by the end of the week.

KEYONNA. Just like that?

Epps, come on.

We paid you.

Yo, you remember that?

We paid you.

EPPS. *(Offstage.)* I'm sorry, aight?

> (*A door slams above.* **OVETTA** *laughs from her perch in the living room, and after a pause,* **KEYONNA** *re-enters the room. A long beat should pass in which* **OVETTA** *is beside herself with laughter. Then she turns to* **KEYONNA**.)

OVETTA. He just mad 'cause he can't get it up.

Never could to be honest.

But you can't say nothin' about it, you know?

Or else his ass get too sensitive!

KEYONNA. What were you even doin' up there, Ma?

OVETTA. Mindin' my business.

Just like you need to mind yours.

> (**OVETTA** *goes into the kitchen and starts to pour herself a glass of water.*)

KEYONNA. The water is off, Ma.

Remember?

> (**KEYONNA** *reaches into her backpack and removes a twenty-ounce bottle of water. She gives it to* **OVETTA**.)

It's my last one 'til tomorrow.

Don't drink it all.

> (**OVETTA** *drinks half the bottle and then stops. She gives it back to* **KEYONNA**. *A pause.*)

What is wrong with you?

OVETTA. –

KEYONNA. I mean...I know what's wrong.

But sometimes I'm just like...what is it really?

OVETTA. I need to lie down.

KEYONNA. No.

Not when I'm tryna talk to you.

OVETTA. I don't feel good, Keyonna.

KEYONNA. Where are we supposed to live, hunh?

If Epps kick us out.

What the fuck are we supposed to do?

OVETTA. I need a minute.

KEYONNA. I'm askin' you a question —

> (**OVETTA** *runs to a trash can and vomits.* **KEYONNA** *takes that in, and then she crosses*

back to her sofa. She stares out while **OVETTA**
gets her bearings.)

KEYONNA. You know when we was kids and you would
fuck up.

Daddy used to say you was havin' an "episode."

Like we was living white folks fancy and we needed to
cover up what it was.

I used to think it was 'cause he watched too many
episodes of *The Nanny.*

Got all that British decency shit mixed up in his head.

But then this one time you came home so drunk and
so low.

You was stumblin' all over the place and you was yellin'
at him.

You was bein so mean,

but the way he looked at you...

I mean he looked at you, and it was like what I was
seein' was the opposite of what he was seein'.

He looked at you like you was his best thing.

Like you was the only thing.

(**OVETTA** *looks over at* **KEYONNA.**)

He loved you so hard.

And I don't think you deserved it.

OVETTA. –

KEYONNA. Go to bed, Ma.

(**KEYONNA** *picks up her notebook and starts
to write again, but then* **OVETTA** *makes a
choice. She crosses to the wall and starts
ripping down the dream board. One by one,*

and with an almost practiced steadiness, **OVETTA** *rips every single photo off the wall.* **KEYONNA** *watches her, a bit too shocked to make a move. Then* **OVETTA** *turns back to her daughter.)*

OVETTA. You don't get to tell me what my marriage was.

KEYONNA. –

OVETTA. You don't get to tell me who I am.

In my house.

When you ain't looked at me like I was somebody in years.

When you ain't even talked to me like —

*(***OVETTA*** *is tripped up by how drunk she is. Maybe she dry heaves. Maybe she almost stumbles. Either way, her drunkenness has caught up to her. She's lost her train of thought.* **KEYONNA** *nods her head, like she's remembering a thought that she tucked away.)*

KEYONNA. I hate you.

OVETTA. You hate me, hunh?

That's all you got?

*(***KEYONNA*** *is silent, taking that in, but then there's a knock on the door. They both turn toward it.* **KEYONNA** *goes to the door.)*

We ain't done here.

*(***KEYONNA*** *opens it. It's* **CHANTEL.***)*

KEYONNA. Shit. No. No.

Now is not a good time.

CHANTEL. Why? What's going on?

OVETTA. You don't get to hate me!

> (**KEYONNA** *looks down.* **CHANTEL** *peers further into the room.*)

You hear me? —

CHANTEL. Yo, Ms. O.

You good.

OVETTA. She don't get to tell me —

> (*Again,* **OVETTA** *is struggling with verbalizing her thoughts.* **CHANTEL** *goes into action mode. She steps past* **KEYONNA,** *drops her backpack, and goes to the older woman.*)

CHANTEL. Let me help you.

OVETTA. I don't need no help.

CHANTEL. Okay, you don't need it.

But what about if I just wanna give it anyway?

OVETTA. –

> (**CHANTEL** *approaches* **OVETTA** *and takes her around the waist.*)

CHANTEL. You good to stand?

You wanna walk with me?

OVETTA. Walk where?

CHANTEL. Your bedroom.

Let's get you to bed.

OVETTA. It ain't nothin' but ten o'clock.

CHANTEL. I know.

But you need your rest, right?

Everybody need a lil' rest.

Come on, Ms. O.

> (**CHANTEL** *guides* **OVETTA** *toward her bedroom. As she does,* **OVETTA** *takes a long look at the younger woman.*)

OVETTA. This kinda like old times, child.

You remember all them years?

> (*They disappear into Ovetta's bedroom.* **KEYONNA** *closes the front door and then simply stands there, processing. After a few beats of this, she crosses to the dream board. She starts picking up the torn cutouts and stacking them in neat piles. She should do this for many moments. Then* **CHANTEL** *enters, closing Ovetta's bedroom door behind her. She approaches* **KEYONNA** *cautiously, taking in the scene.*)

CHANTEL. ...You aight?

> (**KEYONNA** *doesn't respond.*)

Keyonna?

Did...Ms. O do this?

KEYONNA. Yep.

CHANTEL. Shit.

I'm sorry.

KEYONNA. It's cool.

> (*A small pause.*)

CHANTEL. You want some help?

KEYONNA. What are you even doin' here, Chantel?

CHANTEL. –

KEYONNA. Like for real for real.

What do you want now?

CHANTEL. You ain't been in school.

I brought your homework.

KEYONNA. Can you just get out of here, Chantel.

CHANTEL. But Keyonna —

KEYONNA. I can't do this, okay.

I can't do any of this.

CHANTEL. I'm not asking you to do nothin', aight?

I'm just here.

KEYONNA. I don't want you to be here though.

CHANTEL. –

KEYONNA. I just want to pick up my board.

Clean up this mess.

And go to sleep.

CHANTEL. You sure you don't want to talk —

KEYONNA. I'm sure.

CHANTEL. –

KEYONNA. –

CHANTEL. Okay.

> *(She grabs her backpack and then looks back at* **KEYONNA.***)*

I saw Samuel.

I visited him.

KEYONNA. –

CHANTEL. Uh...I told him —

KEYONNA. Good for you.

> (**KEYONNA** *does not look up from her work.* **CHANTEL** *takes that in. Then she crosses to the door and exits. As soon as she does,* **KEYONNA** *breaks open before us. Maybe she doesn't cry, but she lets the real weight of everything that's happened wash over her. After as many moments of this as she needs, she finds the courage. She calls out:)*

Natalie?

> *(Nothing.)*

Hey Natalie, are you here?

Can you...

Will you talk to me?

...

Please.

> (**NATALIE** *enters. She's dressed like a starved and mistreated prisoner in the 1940s: head shaved, badly bruised, anything that evokes her character Evey from* V for Vendetta.*)*

Hi.

NATALIE. Hi.

KEYONNA. It's been a minute.

NATALIE. It has.

> (**KEYONNA** *points at her costume.)*

KEYONNA. That's dramatic as fuck.

NATALIE. You love *V for Vendetta.*

KEYONNA. –

NATALIE. I thought it might make you laugh.

KEYONNA. It is.

On the inside.

> *(A pause.* **NATALIE** *crosses farther into the room.)*

NATALIE. Tell me why you love this one so much.

KEYONNNA. I love the fight scenes.

And the poetry.

Plus, it's the most badass you ever been.

Some people think that was *Black Swan*, but nah.

You ain't had no journey in *Black Swan*.

Just crazy and more crazy.

But in *V for Vendetta*.

You was good first.

And scared.

And lonely.

Then V fucked wit' you.

He was cruel.

And you set it right.

You fought back.

NATALIE. So maybe that's what you need right now?

To fight back.

KEYONNA. What am I supposed to fight with though, Nat?

My fists?

My empty pockets?

NATALIE. With *whatever*.

You're Keyonna.

You can do anything.

You know that.

(*The tiniest pause.*)

KEYONNA. Let's just play a game, okay?

I'll be V, and you'll be Evey.

NATALIE. But Keyonna —

KEYONNA. We'll do that scene right before you blow everything up.

When V's dying.

But his whole plan is coming together.

You remember that one? —

NATALIE. Stop.

(**KEYONNA** *stops.*)

You're sad.

KEYONNA. –

NATALIE. Right?

KEYONNA. No.

NATALIE. You are.

I can see that you are.

KEYONNA. I am not sad, Natalie.

I'm angry.

I'm mad all the fuckin' time.

'Cause nothin' is right.

And nothin' is fair.

And nothin' is the way it's supposed to be.

And I just wish...

> (**KEYONNA** *falters here. This bit is hard, and* **NATALIE** *can see it.*)

I wish my dad was still here.

> (*A small pause.*)

NATALIE. Oh.

You never talk about him.

KEYONNA. Nothing to say.

He was here. Then he wasn't.

It happens I guess, but it's like...

This house used to run like a machine.

A fucked-up machine but still.

We all had a part to play.

Him dying just fucked all our shit up.

And my part was just being me.

Just that.

> (*A pause.* **NATALIE** *just looks at* **KEYONNA**.)

Now is when you cheer me up, Natalie.

NATALIE. The last time I cheered you up didn't go so well.

KEYONNA. I know it didn't but maybe if we just try —

NATALIE. If we try what, Keyonna?

KEYONNA. –

NATALIE. –

KEYONNA. I don't know.

NATALIE. –

KEYONNA. I just want to feel good, you know?

NATALIE. –

KEYONNA. You used to make me feel good.

> *(That hangs. They breathe.* **NATALIE** *racks her brain, trying to find the next salve, but comes up empty.)*
>
> *(Lights.)*

Scene Six

(In darkness, we hear the beeping of a dial tone. Then an automated voice reaches out to us. It's a recording.)

RECORDING. …Hello, this is a collect call from…

SAMUEL. *(Offstage.)* Samuel.

RECORDING. An inmate at a District of Columbia Correctional Facility. If you would like to accept this call and all attending charges, please press —

(The sharp tone of a key being pressed.)

Connecting.

(A light comes up on SAMUEL in a phone booth.)

SAMUEL. Keyonna?

(Nothing.)

Hey.

Key?

(Lights come up on KEYONNA in the living room. She's sorting clothing and other items into a number of large cardboard boxes strewn across the floor. She puts SAMUEL on speakerphone.)

KEYONNA. Hey Sam.

SAMUEL. Shit I thought it didn't put me through.

KEYONNA. Nah I'm here.

Just in the middle of packin'.

SAMUEL. You remember how to pack the trunk?

KEYONNA. Stack the hard-shell stuff like Lincoln logs.

Soft stuff last.

Leave space so the stuff in the back seat can move when we need to sleep.

SAMUEL. And the storage unit —

KEYONNA. I don't think I can do that part, Sam.

Not without nobody strong.

SAMUEL. But all the furniture need to get in there.

We can't lose all our shit.

That's the house.

That's everything —

KEYONNA. I know, but who I'm supposed to ask?

All my make-believe friends?

Ma?

SAMUEL. Just pack that shit up, Key.

I'll get you some help.

(A pause.)

You wanna talk about this school shit?

KEYONNA. Not really.

But I went today.

SAMUEL. And tomorrow?

KEYONNA. I'll go tomorrow too.

SAMUEL. You sure about that?

KEYONNA. I'm sure, Sam.

SAMUEL. Good. Show up. Pass your classes.

KEYONNA. You do realize that passin' my classes is the easy part, right?

SAMUEL. –

KEYONNA. I gotta come home after that and starve.

And fight with Ma.

And miss you.

And think on how much shit I want outta my life that I ain't never gon' have.

SAMUEL. Woah. Hol' up. Why are you talkin' like this?

KEYONNA. 'Cause I'm tired, Sam.

I'm tired every day, and school ain't gon' change that.

It don't change nothin'.

SAMUEL. School change everything, Keyonna.

School a ticket.

KEYONNA. A ticket to where though?

SAMUEL. WHEREVER.

> (*A pause.* **KEYONNA** *focuses on her packing.* **SAMUEL** *makes a decision.*)

Tell me a story, Key.

KEYONNA. Fresh outta stories.

SAMUEL. You ain't never been fresh out of a story in your life.

KEYONNA. First time for everything, right?

SAMUEL. *Keyonna.*

KEYONNA. –

SAMUEL. Talk to me.

> (**KEYONNA** *takes a breath, but then she begins.*)

KEYONNA. Once there was an old lady.

...

The oldest lady in the history of the universe.

And she lived in this tiny lil' shack...four walls crumbling...door hangin' off the hinge.

Windows busted.

And she ain't had a cent to her name.

But whenever you saw her, no matter the season, the time of day, you name it...she was happy.

No matter who she ran into, this old lady was smilin' like today was the best day. And she just knew tomorrow would be even better.

Like her and time had a secret that nobody else was in on.

Like she was ready for anything.

But then...one day in her 187th year...the sun didn't rise.

That morning she sat up in bed like usual.

She put on her glasses. And she looked out her bedside window.

Only the sky she saw was dark.

The whole world was dark as far as her old eyes could see.

And suddenly, for the first time ever, for the first time anyone could remember, the lil' old lady cried.

She sat right there in her bed and she just cried for the whole goddamn universe.

(*A long pause.*)

SAMUEL. You never told me that one before.

KEYONNA. That's because it's new.

You like it?

SAMUEL. Not really.

KEYONNA. Yeah well.

(A pause.)

SAMUEL. Key, I'm gon' say somethin' to you.

KEYONNA. –

SAMUEL. And I ain't sayin' it 'cause I feel guilty, aight?

I'm sayin' it 'cause you clearly need to hear it.

KEYONNA. –

SAMUEL. I stole that money from Lee.

KEYONNA. –

SAMUEL. I skimmed off the register for weeks.

Because I needed it.

'Cause we needed it.

To cover the small shit, you know?

KEYONNA. –

SAMUEL. That's what's messed about bein' us, Key.

We gotta do fucked-up shit just to get through.

We gotta feel fucked-up shit every day.

But that don't mean the sky ain't got no sun in it.

Just mean we still fightin'.

(A pause.)

Key, you still there?

KEYONNA. I'm here.

SAMUEL. I'm sorry, aight?

For the money.

For this shit with Chantel. // It's all so messy.

KEYONNA. I don't wanna talk about her, Sam.

I just wanna pack and keep it movin' —

SAMUEL. Let me just get this out, Keyonna.

> *(A pause.)*

…I'm sorry for knowin'.

For knowin' this whole time and still goin' after her.

KEYONNA. Whatchu mean knowin'?

SAMUEL. Just…you always had a way of lookin' at her.

A way of talkin' to her, you know?

But I guess when y'all stopped coolin', I forgot all that.

I chose to forget all that.

And I moved on her.

But I shouldn'ta done that.

KEYONNA. –

SAMUEL. I just needed somethin' for me, Key.

I feel like ever since Daddy died, I been carryin' all this shit around with me.

Shit that ain't even mine.

It's Ma's.

And Lee's.

And yours.

And all my stuff just left on the side of the road.

…But Chantel.

She make shit better, you know?

She light.

And I'on know I just wanted that feelin'.

You so good at findin' it. Key.

And I just —

KEYONNA. It's fine, Sam.

I don't need her —

SAMUEL. Maybe you do.

Maybe you don't.

KEYONNA. –

SAMUEL. Just know that you got my blessing either way, sis.

I ain't in the business of blocking your shine.

KEYONNA. But what about your shine, Sam?

SAMUEL. Girl, don't you know I glisten?

I fuckin' glow in the dark with my shit —

KEYONNA. Ohmygod.

Nerd —

SAMUEL. I love you, Key.

KEYONNA. –

SAMUEL. If you don't hold on to nothing else.

Hold on to that.

>   *(A breath between them.)*
>
>   *(Lights.)*

Scene Seven

(The apartment the following night. Pretty much everything in the apartment has been boxed up or moved out, but the kitchen is still untackled. In fact, the kitchen is occupied. By **OVETTA.** *Who stands over a number of pots and pans, inspecting their contents. After a few beats of her stirring and fretting, the front door opens. It's* **KEYONNA,** *who carries a few cardboard boxes and tape. Upon entering, she spots her mother, smells the air, and just sort of stands there in disbelief.* **OVETTA** *turns to her. They take one another in. Then* **OVETTA** *turns off the various pots and pans.)*

OVETTA. Before you say anything.

I don't care if you ate that Safeway food.

I cooked. It's ready. And I wanna feed you.

One last time under this roof.

KEYONNA. You were supposed to pack up the kitchen, Ma.

Not cook in it —

OVETTA. And I will pack it up.

Soon as you eat.

KEYONNA. –

OVETTA. Anyway, I only cooked the stuff that might go bad.

All the dry goods already out in the car —

KEYONNA. I'm not hungry.

OVETTA. Keyonna come on now.

KEYONNA. And you shoulda just done what I asked you instead of wastin' time —

OVETTA. Keyonna *please.*

KEYONNA. –

OVETTA. I went to all this trouble.

> *(A pause.)*

KEYONNA. ...Whatchu make?

OVETTA. Some collards and some rice and beans.

KEYONNA. You make the collards with the —

OVETTA. Rosemary and garlic? Yeah.

I know how you like it.

KEYONNA. Where you get the rosemary?

OVETTA. Epps had some up there.

If you can believe it.

KEYONNA. Epps?

He talkin' to you now?

OVETTA. For five minutes, yeah.

Best he could do seein' as I apologized to his triflin' ass.

KEYONNA. You? Apologized?

OVETTA. Gotta play my cards right, don't I?

Without him we ain't got no references for our housing applications so...

KEYONNA. You think Epps gon' say nice things about us.

OVETTA. I think I'm workin' on him.

KEYONNA. What kind of workin' on him?

OVETTA. I'm talkin' to him, Keyonna.

Just talkin'.

> *(A pause.)*

Look.

About your board.

Your pictures.

KEYONNA. It's cool —

OVETTA. No, it is not cool.

KEYONNA. –

OVETTA. I shouldn'ta done that.

I was just so far gone.

And you...you upset me.

KEYONNA. You upset me too, Ma.

You realize that right?

OVETTA. I do.

KEYONNA. So why do it?

Why pick at me?

Why blame me? —

OVETTA. I don't blame you for nothin', babygirl.

I don't.

It's just...sometimes it's so easy to get mad. So easy to only see the shit that make you feel small.

KEYONNA. You sayin' I make you feel small?

OVETTA. I'm sayin' that I realize I can't just blame it on the bottle.

It's me.

I don't reach for you right.

You across the room, and I just reach for you all wrong.

KEYONNA. –

OVETTA. But I wanna do better, aight?

I wanna try and understand you.

> *(A pause.* **OVETTA** *proceeds to make her daughter a plate of food.)*

Lord.

Seem like all we do is upset each other nowadays.

But I remember when it was the opposite.

You remember?

KEYONNA. That was a long time ago, Ma.

> *(They lapse into silence for a moment. But then* **OVETTA** *reaches into her pocket, retrieves a small silver coin, and presents it to* **KEYONNA.***)*

What is that?

OVETTA. It's a sobriety chip.

From AA.

KEYONNA. –

OVETTA. I went to a meeting today.

Two actually.

Nice folks.

Sad.

But nice.

And they give me this.

> *(***KEYONNA** *takes the chip and inspects it.)*

See?

Twenty-four hours sober.

KEYONNA. –

OVETTA. Woman who give it to me say she my sponsor now.

Me and her had a long talk.

We shared stuff with each other.

Information.

I told her about your father passin'.

How much it wrecked me.

How much it wrecked all us.

And they know all about that kinda thing —

KEYONNA. Why are you telling me this, Ma?

OVETTA. Because this house is broken, Keyonna.

Because I'm broken.

But you ain't.

Not yet I don't think.

> *(She sits beside* **KEYONNA.***)*

This way of livin' ain't all there is, babygirl.

You taught me that.

So, don't you dare lose sight of that.

Don't you give up.

Just keep on doin' what you do, and I promise I'll be here to help carry the weight.

KEYONNA. –

OVETTA. That is.

If you'll still have me?

> *(***KEYONNA** *just looks at her mother.* **OVETTA** *just looks back. Then, when she's ready...)*

KEYONNA. Of course, I'll have you.

(A tender pause. Maybe **OVETTA** *grips* **KEYONNA***'s hand. Then they recover.)*

OVETTA. Look at us.

Talkin' and spendin' time.

KEYONNA. –

OVETTA. I like it.

I miss it.

And we gon' keep doin' it.

KEYONNA. –

OVETTA. Startin' with watchin' us a movie tonight.

KEYONNA. With what TV?

OVETTA. This one here.

(She lifts a small, handheld DVD player from somewhere hidden.)

Got it at the pawn shop on H Street.

It's handheld. And the buttons don't work right.

But it play DVDs just fine.

KEYONNA. –

OVETTA. I already took the liberty of puttin' in *Mighty Joe Young.*

KEYONNA. I love that movie.

OVETTA. Yes, you do.

Almost as much as them damn pigtails.

(A small pause.)

KEYONNA. Okay.

Let's do it.

(**OVETTA** *starts to power on the DVD player, but then there's a knock on the door.* **KEYONNA** *moves for it, but* **OVETTA** *stops her.*)

OVETTA. Naw, you sit and eat. I got it.

(*She goes to the door and opens it. It's* **CHANTEL.**)

Hm.

I thought you might make your way back here tonight.

CHANTEL. Is she home yet?

OVETTA. Yeah.

She here.

(*She steps aside.* **CHANTEL** *and* **KEYONNA** *can see one another now.* **OVETTA** *closes the door.*)

Well.

I expect we can watch our movie in the mornin', Keyonna.

Might be hilarious to watch it in the car with all our shit.

Homeless but happy.

(**OVETTA** *goes to her bedroom door, but pauses as she does. She considers the two young women. Then she closes the bedroom door.* **KEYONNA** *sets aside her plate of food and stands, but before she can say anything,* **CHANTEL** *begins.*)

CHANTEL. Look, I know I ain't been the most consistent with all this.

I know I been...confused...and I hurt you.

And I hurt Sam.

But...it's only 'cause I was scared.

KEYONNA. Scared of what?

CHANTEL. Of you.

...You terrify me.

KEYONNA. How?

CHANTEL. I don't know. You just do.

KEYONNA. Humor me, Chantel.

Try puttin' it into words.

(*A pause.*)

CHANTEL. I don't know...you just...

KEYONNA. –

CHANTEL. You know that scene in *Love and Basketball*?

KEYONNA. Which one?

CHANTEL. When Monica and Quincy meet in the cut between they houses.

And they known each other they whole lives.

And cared for each other that whole time.

But on that night...for some reason...somethin' in the air is just different.

Somethin' between them is just...different.

Or maybe it's the same?

I don't know.

They was the best of friends for so long and then all of a sudden they just this other thing.

This *big* thing.

Monica just look so scared in that scene, Key.

She standin' right in front of this dude she *been* knowin', but she quakin'.

And I get that.

Because that's how I feel when you look at me.

Sometimes.

>*(A pause.* **CHANTEL** *isn't sure if what she said made any sense. But* **KEYONNA** *takes it in.)*

KEYONNA. You hungry, Chantel?

CHANTEL. I'm starvin'. Why?

>*(A breath between them.)*

>*(Lights shift.)*

Scene Eight

(We see a parked car. Somehow we can see into the back seat where **OVETTA** *and* **KEYONNA** *sit side by side.* **KEYONNA** *holds the DVD player. We hear muffled orchestrations that signal the ending of a very good movie.* **KEYONNA** *is near tears, but* **OVETTA** *is fast asleep.* **KEYONNA** *closes the DVD player and starts to get comfortable, but then the hood of the car creaks beneath the weight of something.* **KEYONNA** *peers around, confused for a moment, but then we can suddenly see the hood of the car.* **NATALIE** *sits there. She's dressed like a precocious young girl, likely evoking her character Mathilda in* The Professional. *She's relaxed, and she peers up at the night sky.* **KEYONNA** *opens the car door, hops atop the hood, and sits beside* **NATALIE**. *They simply stare up at the stars for a long beat. Then* **KEYONNA** *breaks the silence.)*

KEYONNA. *The Professional*, hunh?

We takin' it all the way back?

NATALIE. It felt right.

My first big splash on the silver screen!

Your first big splash on the —

KEYONNA. On the homeless circuit?

Damn, Nat. That's cold.

NATALIE. Ohmygod. That is so not what I meant.

I just meant...you know.

Life.

It's happening.

KEYONNA. *(Gestures around.)* I don't know if I'd call *this* happening.

But yeah.

...I guess so.

>   *(A pause.)*

NATALIE. She's pretty.

If I haven't said so.

KEYONNA. I know she's pretty.

>   *(A pause. They look at one another.)*

NATALIE. How about a game?

KEYONNA. You wanna turn *The Professional* into a game?

Literally so many people die in that movie —

NATALIE. ...Just a short one.

For me.

>   *(A pause. Then **KEYONNA** makes a decision. As **KEYONNA** tells this story, maybe they act it out in some small-scale physical way.)*

KEYONNA. There's a scene near the end.

I play Leon — the hitman — and I'm holdin' a machine gun, right?

NATALIE. So many machine guns.

KEYONNA. And these dirty cops are at the door with their guns cocked too, and the shit is about to go down. Full-scale shoot-out!

NATALIE. The drama!

KEYONNA. So, I pause, and I focus on you — this little girl who has become like my best friend in the whole entire world — I pick you up and I put you in this hole in the wall so you can escape.

KEYONNA. I set you free.

NATALIE. –

KEYONNA. But before I do that, I tell you the thing I been wanting to say the whole movie.

And it's a creepy thing to say 'cause I'm a grown-ass man and you like twelve —

NATALIE. Keyonna —

KEYONNA. I tell you what I been wantin' to say.

And then you just…go.

Wherever it is you go.

NATALIE. –

KEYONNA. I could do that now.

If you want me to.

NATALIE. I do.

KEYONNA. Thank you, Natalie.

NATALIE. –

KEYONNA. For everything.

For listening.

> (**NATALIE** *smiles wide. Then, as if she can't bear to remain any longer,* **NATALIE** *goes. A long pause should pass in which* **KEYONNA** *just watches the spot where Natalie was. But then the moon appears in the sky. It's big, and bright, and vibrant. It's almost as if* **KEYONNA** *has found her own private sun. She takes it in, the moon, and the stars, and the whole goddamn universe.)*

> (*Blackout.*)

End of Play

CPSIA information can be obtained
at www.ICGtesting.com
Printed in the USA
BVHW051714050123
655646BV00013B/870

9 780573 709524